GUARDIANS OF THE MORTAL REALM

SHAY LEE GIERTZ

Late November

GUARDIANS OF THE MORTAL REALM
By Shay Lee Giertz

Published by Late November Literary
Winston Salem, NC 27107

ISBN (Print): 979-8-9892723-1-0
Copyright 2023 by Shay Lee Giertz
Cover design by Sweet N' Spicy designs
Interior design by Late November Literary

Available in print or online. Visit latenovemberliterary.com.

Library of Congress Cataloging-in-Publication data
Giertz, Shay Lee.
Guardians of the Mortal Realm / Shay Lee Giertz 1st ed.

Printed in the United States of America

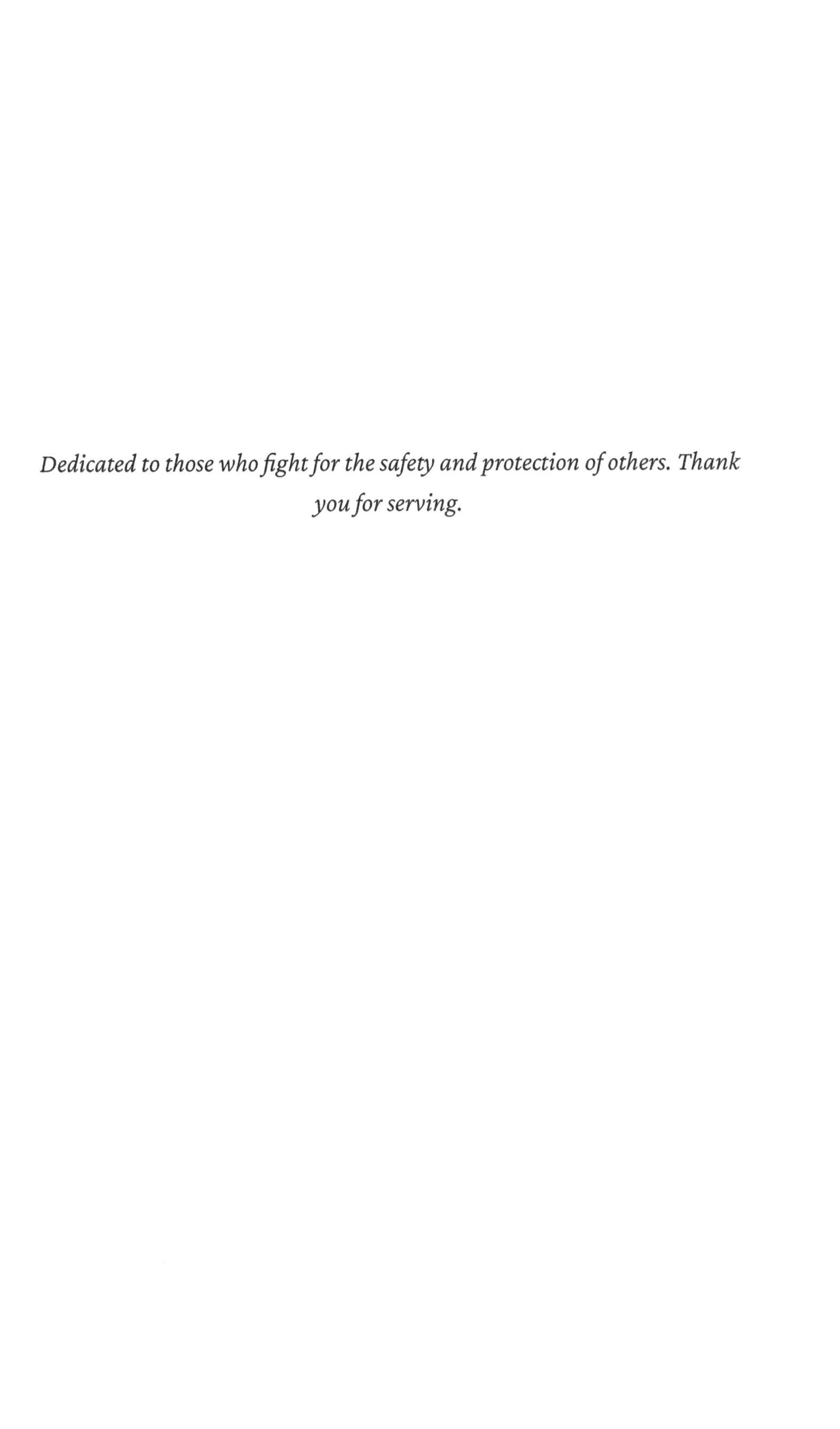

Dedicated to those who fight for the safety and protection of others. Thank you for serving.

"Behold, I make all things new."
Revelation 21:5

1

KRAAL

The cellar was old and musty. Spiderwebs and mice droppings were the only signs of life. Until two Shadows emerged from a dark corner.

They found a spot behind abandoned boxes and huddled together, both shaking in fear. Their death was imminent. So, they waited and listened. Because at some point Drakkon, the devil himself, would show up and disintegrate them into nothing but piles of ash.

The younger Shadow, merely a trainee, whimpered and held her stomach. "I feel sick," she whispered to the older Shadow.

"Shh," he said, bringing his finger to his lips.

But the young Shadow trainee could no longer hold it in. Rancid bile poured out of her. She vomited until there was nothing left. She broke out in a cold sweat, as the older Shadow moved her to a different part of the cellar. "I'm sorry." The girl could barely say the words, as another wave of nausea hit.

"It's the mortal realm," the older Shadow whispered. "You've been here too long. The purge will only get worse the longer you're here."

"I can't go back." She began to whimper again. "What are we going to do, Kraal?"

"I don't know. There's no turning back from this. If Marcy doesn't help us, we won't survive." Kraal studied the young girl's face. She had dirty blonde hair with two braids dangling and long bangs to cover the trademark Shadow feature: black orbs for eyes. Other than for her eyes, she looked like a typical thirteen-year-old human. One that had been badly beaten. Her one arm had been burnt off and thrown in the inferno. Her only crime was knowing Marcy. Drakkon used their friendship to lure Marcy to sign his book with her blood.

"Did you see the way she flew in the air? It was the most majestic thing I've ever seen." The girl leaned her head against the filthy cellar wall. "She'll come for us. I know it."

"I'm not so sure," Kraal said. "She's a light-bearer. We are from hell. We don't exactly mix." All Shadows were descendants from the mortal world, but they were also agents of hell. Meant to manipulate the thoughts of mortals. It was because of Shadows that mankind was so bitter, angry, and unhappy. And light cannot mix with darkness, which meant that Kraal and this girl might be on their own.

He remembered the day Marcy came to him. She was Deborah then: a powerful light-bearer and furious that he had stolen the baby. The human child was an anomaly with divine powers of both mortal and spirit realms. Deborah had been sent to protect the child, but Kraal had stolen him first. He had to play his hand right. If he could make this angel see the torture that he and other Shadows endured in hell, maybe she would have mercy and help set them free. "Let me explain," he had begged after she had easily pinned him down and had her sword to his chest.

"Where is he?"

"We need help. Please, I beg for mercy." Kraal saw the hesitation in her eyes. As a light-bearer, she provided mercy whenever asked with sincerity. He was glad she heard the sincerity of his words.

"Provide me the child, and then we'll speak of mercy."

"He's gone. Drakkon snatched him as soon as he found out I had him."

"Take me to him. I demand the child and will tear down hell's gates to retrieve him."

"But he'll kill the baby. He won't let you have him."

She yelled in frustration, releasing Kraal from her hold. Instead, she paced the forest floor.

"Please. I have an idea. I can get you into hell, but you'll have to do as I say."

"Convenient. Are you just coming up with this? Making a deal with a light-bearer? You even ask for mercy."

"You know what I say is true, which is why you haven't already ripped through hell's gates. And I have spent much time seeking freedom. I may be from hell, but trust me, I know that true freedom can only come from you."

"I need the child. Tell me your plan and make it quick. We are wasting precious seconds."

"Disguise yourself."

"Even disguising myself will not last long. Light repels darkness."

"You'll have to be reborn. I can get you into hell, but you will be part human. The humanity will disguise the light within you."

"And where will I go in hell if I am an infant? I will have to wait years to bring him back where he belongs. And if he is killed anyway? Then I'm stuck in hell." Her face showed her disgust.

"What choice do you have? You will have to trust me. I will place you in the safest place. It's called Levea. It's where all Shadow infants are born. That way I can personally watch over you. When the time is right, we will work together to bring him back to you."

She groaned in frustration again. "And why should I trust you? Nothing from hell is good. It is tainted with the darkest of evils."

"Like I said, what choice do you have?"

"I need to talk to Michael."

"That's up to you, but you're wasting precious seconds."

"Let's do it quickly." She took the elixir Kraal had snatched from Drakkon's stash. She studied it for a second, then said, "Everything for a purpose."

Kraal had stayed true to his word and watched over the infant shadow, making sure she was put in the least vile of factions, providing her leniency for her mortal possessions. He also watched the infant boy who Drakkon had taken as his own.

He wasn't surprised that Marcy had actually been successful in retrieving Tor. But now what? Was it all for nothing? Would she forget about him and the Shadows who were still slaves to the demons of hell?

Kraal felt the nausea and knew a purge was coming. He'd lasted longer than Mathilde, but even he couldn't stay in the mortal realm for too long without purging. If he had his way, he'd stay in the mortal realm forever. He'd stay anywhere to simply get out of hell.

But who would save him? Just the thought of Marcy not finding them brought a wave of hopelessness upon him. He cried out, and then turned from the girl and retched.

Tor was in a bad mood.

He didn't know which bothered him more: getting beat to a bloody pulp by Drakkon, having absolutely no powers to protect himself from anything or anyone, finding out that the first woman he ever loved was in love with not just anyone but with an archangel, or being barely able to stand in an upright position in negative temperatures in what seemed to be the top of a giant mountain.

Tor's training in the spirit realm had taken place in hell. He was used to heat. But his tolerance for heat did not come in handy in the frigid weather conditions of whatever mountain top in whatever region Michael dumped him off at. He stood there shivering while Michael went inside some small opening in the snow-covered rock in front of them. "I'm human, you know," Tor said through chattering teeth. Not that Michael listened.

"Me too," Timothy said good-naturedly. "But we won't be out

here long. Michael knows what he's doing." He unwrapped his scarf and gently wrapped it around Tor's neck. Timothy was fully decked out in a snow suit so thick he looked like he'd been stuffed with pillows. "I've been to a place like this before, so I came prepared. Most of their secret places here on earth are tucked near mountain tops. My abbey is the only location that I know of that is relatively close to any type of human activity. And even then, there's only one road that leads to it, many kilometers from others. Unfortunately, I didn't have a lot of extra winter clothes for you."

Tor had been given a coat, gloves, and hat, but that did little against wind so cold it stabbed at his legs and face. The scarf brought some relief as Tor covered his ears with it. A thank you sat on his tongue, but it felt foreign in his mouth. He wasn't used to gratitude. He also wasn't used to company, especially when that company was friendly and his mortal father. He looked away, still awkward at the knowledge of who the man was.

When Michael had told him the priest in the Irish abbey was his biological father, Tor had acted dumbfounded. Then again, he was still healing from Drakkon's attack.

Was it merely hours ago he had nearly died at the hands of Drakkon? What irony it would be if it was cold that took his life.

If only I had his powers. He thought longingly of forcing the clouds to move aside and let the sun come through. He'd end the snow and blustery wind. If only he still controlled fire, he'd be toasty in no time. But nope. None of that. Just a weak, pathetic, freezing human.

Michael emerged from the small opening in the rock and motioned for them to follow him.

"Do you need help?" Timothy asked, taking Tor's arm and draping it around his shoulders. "Lean on me. I won't let you fall."

Tor didn't want his help, but he found himself leaning on his father as they moved slowly against the frosty wind to where Michael stood. The movement shot pain throughout his body, and Tor winced with each step.

"Can you make it the rest of the way?" Michael asked. "I can carry you."

"I'd rather die," Tor muttered.

Michael smiled at Tor's insult. "Glad to see your sarcasm didn't get injured."

The warmth enveloped Tor, and he found himself breathing a sigh of relief. He also felt the powerful energy. The same energy that engulfed Eli's forest surrounding the abbey. His insides no longer shook, and his teeth no longer chattered.

The passageway seemed long and never-ending. Timothy helped him walk through what appeared to be dim tunnels. But Michael led the way, his light breaking through the darkness. The archangel needed no torch or anything else to light the way, and he didn't act lost. Tor glanced behind him only to see pitch dark. "What is this place?"

"To humans, it is a cave near the top of the mountain. Most mortals do not have the ability or wherewithal to access so high an altitude. However, if anyone does, it's nothing more than a cave."

Michael abruptly stopped. Someone approached. Tor had to look up to take in the sight of the enormous man who stood before them. And Tor had thought Michael looked intimidating. Even this guy's neck had muscles. But his muscular stature didn't captivate

Tor for long. It was his eyes or lack thereof. They were completely gone with his eyelids sewed shut covering the sockets.

"Does he agree to the oath?" The man's deep voice reverberated along the passageway. The blind man looked from Michael to Tor, which felt odd since he literally had no eyeballs. "Do you agree to the oath? You cannot enter otherwise."

"Can he see me?" Tor whispered to Timothy.

"Yes," the man answered before Timothy could. "In ways you have yet to understand. I can also hear you. Now, answer the question. Do you agree to the oath or not?"

"I did not tell him about the oath. He needed to get out of the cold. He is human," Michael answered.

The giant still kept his attention on Tor, and Tor was riveted. His current pain momentarily forgotten. "What oath?" he asked.

"It is a sacred vow of my kind. No alcohol of any kind, no touching of any dead thing, and no razor to your head."

Tor felt the temptation to laugh at such bizarre requests until he noticed the man's long hair. "It's to your waist."

"The power that is to be bestowed upon you comes at a high price, but the power is yours if you get the proper training. If I train you, you must agree to the Nazarite covenant."

Tor considered his current situation, then muttered, "What choice do I have? I'm barely standing, and I need somewhere to get my strength back, somewhere away from... never mind. Yes, I'll agree to the oath."

"There is always a choice," the man said. He took a small knife and made a slight cut into his palm. Then he extended his hand. "If you so choose, then swear to the oath by a blood covenant."

Since he heavily leaned on Timothy with his right side, Tor extended his left hand.

"No. It must be your right hand."

Timothy moved to the other side of Tor, helping Tor lean his weight upon him. Just that act alone had Tor's legs shaking with fatigue. He felt he would collapse at any moment. Still, he extended his right hand. The man handed him the blade. "The blood oath must be initiated by your own hand."

Tor sighed in frustration. "I am about to fall over. You obviously can't see that I am in serious pain and need medical attention."

"Yes, I can see that. I can see that seven of your ribs are bruised, one is broken. I can also see that you have suffered severe blunt-force trauma to your organs with some internal bleeding, not to mention the extensive wounds and bruising to your face and your extremities. Your nose is broken, and you can barely see out your one eye because the other is still swollen." He pushed the small knife at Tor. "But the blood oath must come from your hand. Then you can receive the rest, training, and attention you seek."

Gritting his teeth, Tor stood without assistance. He broke out into a cold sweat, and as quickly as he could, took the knife and made a small cut into his palm. A trickle of blood immediately came to the surface. He stuck his hand out, and the large man clasped his own palm to Tor's.

"The covenant is now in place."

As soon as the words left the man's mouth, a jolt of energy shot through Tor. Images and memories flooded through him, not just his own but this light-bearer's memories too. He sucked in a shocked breath as an incredible power pulsated through him.

"Steady," the man said, not letting of his grip. "Take deep breaths. In and out."

But Tor could only stare at this man who now appeared glowing with his eyes in their rightful place. "Your eyes…" Tor tried to regulate his breathing.

Both the man and Michael smiled knowingly at Tor. "I told you I could see," the man said and gave Tor a wink. "Now, say your good-byes and let me take you to your dwelling."

Tor could still feel the powerful energy thrumming through his veins. His legs no longer shook from pain and fatigue, and it no longer hurt to breathe. Whatever this man could teach him, Tor was ready to follow and learn. Yet, he hesitated. He made eye contact with Timothy and saw his pained expression.

"I was hopeful," Timothy began, "What I mean to say is that I am hoping to stay with my son. We have just been reconciled, and I desire to stay here." He looked at Michael for assistance. "Please."

"This is not what was agreed upon," the large light-bearer said. "If Tor is to train, he can have no distractions."

"I will not be a distraction, sir. I can't bear the thought of saying good-bye when I just was introduced to him." Timothy pressed his lips together.

Tor had numerous emotions bubbling through him, especially since stepping away from hell. Drakkon made it his mission to beat any emotion or feeling out of Tor. It now all felt overwhelming. But he understood Timothy's sentiments. His father wanted to be with his only son. A son who he thought was gone forever. "Could he take the oath?" The words came out of Tor's mouth before he could talk himself out of it. "If he took the oath, then he could come with me."

"I will gladly take the oath," Timothy said and extended his hand.

"The oath is not for you," Michael said to Timothy, his words full of compassion. "It is a sacred covenant, and individuals are chosen for it."

"I do not have to be chosen to follow the rules of the oath. I will follow the Nazarite covenant for as long as I have breath in my lungs. I make this vow before God." The air shifted at Timothy's words. Tor felt it. Whatever was buzzing inside him intensified as if in approval.

Michael and the large man must have sensed it too because they quickly glanced at each other and simultaneously raised their eyebrows. "Let it be so," the light-bearer said. He took the small blade and handed it to Timothy. Timothy made a small cut in his palm and extended his hand. "Not with me. You are making this pact with your son. If either of you fail in any way, the impact will be generational."

Timothy extended his hand in Tor's direction. Before Tor clasped his hand, Michael stepped forward. "Both of you need to understand that all of Tor's experiences will be shared with Timothy." To Timothy, he added, "You need to brace yourself. Tor has over twenty years of memories from the darkest corners of hell. The average human has no idea the depths of such darkness."

"Will it kill him?" Tor wasn't about to let his father die.

"The light now within you will most likely drown out the darkness, but it will still be felt. I want to make sure Timothy understands this. We are not sure the ramifications."

"If my son experienced it, then I want to know. Please, son, let me make this oath with you." Timothy's hand stayed in place, and his eyes pleaded with Tor.

Tor took a deep breath and clasped hands with his father. Immediately, Timothy dropped to his knees, yet his grip stayed tight. He trembled and shrieked. Tor tried to release him, realizing too late that it would be too much for his father, but Timothy's grip was like iron. Tor watched as Timothy's eyes rolled in the back of his head and listened to his whimpers. It was too much. "Make it stop," Tor pleaded. "Don't let him endure this."

"It's his choice," Michael said in concern. "He can let go at any time."

Timothy released Tor's hand and crumpled the rest of the way to the ground. He openly wept, and his trembling had yet to abate. Tor looked at Michael and the other to receive any direction, but they acted almost as uneasy as Tor. "Can you carry him to my dwelling?" Tor asked. "I can look after him there."

"You need to fully heal," the light-bearer said. "The light within you will spread over time, and it has definitely given you strength, but the job isn't complete. I'll see that he recovers." He bent down and picked up Timothy like he might pick up a sack of flour. To Michael, he said, "Good-bye, brother. They have taken the oath and will be protected and trained here."

Michael nodded, then turned to Tor. "I look forward to the next time we meet."

Tor glanced away, not ready to say the same thing. Instead, he said, "Make sure to keep my location a secret." Tor couldn't have distractions, and that meant saying good-bye forever to the only person he ever loved. It meant never again seeing the woman who stole his heart and saved his life even when he had tried to kill her.

"I understand," Michael said.

They left Michael in the passageway. Tor was glad for renewed strength. It felt incredible whatever it was that pulsated within him. The pain had completely disappeared. Tor followed the bulky guy carrying his father with little discomfort. "How far do these tunnels go?"

"Far."

Timothy had gone back from whimpering to fully weeping. It unnerved Tor. He needed conversation to drown it out. "Are you a light-bearer like Michael?"

"A light-bearer? Is that what you call it?" The man chuckled. "Michael is an archangel. He leads the host of the Most High's army. I am not an archangel. I was like you. A human."

"How'd you get to be here? And if you're not an archangel, what are you?"

"I guess you can say that I'm a guardian. So, is Eli. There are many of us. Here to protect creation from its enemy."

"I was the enemy," Tor said quietly. "I hated earth and the mortals."

"No, you didn't. You were told to hate it, and you complied. But it wasn't hate that saved the boy and his mother from the tsunami."

"You know about that?"

"Yes. When we clasped hands, I learned everything about you. You saved people's lives on more than one occasion."

"I killed many human lives too. The natural disasters I wrought had devasting consequences for millions."

"Yes, that is true too."

Tor remembered some of the horrible commands he carried out with Drakkon beside him. Hurricanes and electrical storms were used often. His attention turned back to his father still crying. "The same thing that happened to Timothy happened to you? He now knows all about me?"

"Yes, but I anticipated it, not that it would have the same effect on me. I am, as you say, a light-bearer."

"Why didn't I receive information about Timothy's life?"

"You did, but you have yet to learn how to use the light within you, and let's be honest, you were more concerned about Timothy. If you get a chance to focus on what happened, you will find everything you need to know about your father. It's in you now."

"Will this be a part of my training?"

"Enough questions. We're almost there."

"Can I at least know your name?"

"Don't you know it yet? You have the answers inside of you."

Tor concentrated, but all the events blurred together into one never-ending source of energy. He sighed. "I got nothing."

"My name is Samson," the man said.

3

KRAAL

Mortal hours passed, making Kraal feel like a caged animal. The cellar was small and enclosed, and every available corner had been used for retching.

"I'm thirsty," Mathilde said. "I know we shouldn't go into the house, but my throat is on fire."

Kraal stood up weakly just as ready to get out of the cellar that now stank of Shadow vomit. "The house is empty, but we cannot travel through the shadows. It's the easiest way to be tracked."

The two of them climbed up the steps. Kraal slowly opened the cellar door. His skills as a Master Shadow did come in handy because he had the ability to read the situation from a large radius. He didn't want to use shadow transport, but sensing signs and reading minds couldn't be shut off. It was as much a part of him as breathing. "There is no water to the house," he said, not hearing any working pipes. "But there is a well out behind the shed. I saw it on our way here."

"We'll have to be in the open?"

"There's nothing close to pose a threat. My guess is that Drakkon is a little busy at the moment to be too worried about us."

"It'd be nice if he forgot us forever."

"He won't, Mathilde. He never forgets, never forgives, and always seeks vengeance. But I don't sense him or anything at all. We found a good location in the middle of nowhere." He sensed Mathilde's hesitation. "I can go and see if there is some way to bring water back here."

"No, I want to get out of this cellar."

"All right, then. Follow me."

The two moved in the darkness to the well. Kraal noticed the lightening of the eastern sky. Sunrise was imminent.

They reached the dilapidated shed with its door barely hanging on. "Look for a bucket or anything that can hold water. I'll get the well primed." Mathilde hesitated again; her fear palpable. "No one is around. I'd be able to sense it."

She nodded and slipped into the shed. Kraal kept going to the well and began to pump it. Unfortunately, Shadows were no stronger than mortals, so he had to use all his strength to get the pump moving. He heard Mathilde approach, but he didn't stop pumping. "No bucket. The shed was empty," she said to him. "Any luck with the water?"

"Not yet, but it's coming. I can feel it." As soon as Kraal spoke the words, a tiny stream of water trickled out of the spigot. He rarely had reason to smile, but a small one came to his features. Soon the pump was gushing water.

Mathilde fell to her knees and drank the water with her mouth wide open. Kraal thought about telling her to wait a few minutes to make sure the water was clean, but if her throat was on fire like his was, then he understood. She guzzled and guzzled the cold liquid while Kraal pumped. He needed to drink too.

"Your turn." Mathilde pushed herself up and went to Kraal. "I'll use my one good arm."

Kraal gave one big push of the pump and fell to his knees to drink right from the spigot. The relief to his parched throat was immediate. Mathilde struggled with the same speed and intensity, but she was able to pump the water with her one good arm and her body weight. Kraal drank some more, then let it wash over his face. Shadows did not normally need water. When in the spirit realm, their bodies adjusted and adapted to the environment. It was one of the reasons Shadows couldn't stay in the mortal realm for long. Their human side could take over and desire the comforts of the mortal realm that fed the flesh.

But the mortal realm was simply amazing. Eating and drinking were such pleasures, and Shadows often indulged whenever possible. There was no water or food in hell, and no Shadow dared smuggle it. Well, other than Marcy, but Kraal had made sure she stayed under the radar of nosy demons and ruthless Guardians. Marcy was fearless. Then again, she was a light-bearer trapped in a human body. Kraal hadn't known what to expect but having her in hell changed everything for him. And it changed everything for the other Shadows too. He saw it. They were no longer content as slaves.

"Look," Mathilde said, stopping and pointing at the early sun's rays lighting up the eastern sky.

Kraal sat back on his feet and observed it in awe. This. This is what he desired most of all. To watch every sunrise and sunset and simply marvel. He had never dared to hope, and oh, how he struggled with jealousy. The mortals had no idea just how incredible these miracles were. They barely glanced at nature. But if Kraal was ever given a chance, he'd bask in the miracle of life that flowed through the mortal realm every moment.

"Have you ever seen anything so beautiful?" Mathilde asked. It was evident this was the first time for her. As a Shadow trainee, her schedule was regimented and only included the mortal realm during night hours. "I'll be right back. I still need to look for that bucket."

"I thought you said you didn't find one?"

"I didn't look. I was too thirsty. Be right back."

Before Kraal could answer, he felt the shift in the atmosphere. He jumped up so fast, it startled Mathilde. "We're not alone," he barely whispered.

The wonder on Mathilde's face immediately changed to panic. "What do we do?"

"Go to the shed and stay there. I don't want anyone finding you." When Mathilde stayed beside him, he whispered. "Trust me. The shed is probably the safest place. Don't come out until I come to you."

She moved quickly to the shed. Kraal surveyed the landscape, but nothing stuck out to him. Something fell from the sky, landing in front of him. Not something…someone. Kraal stared at the light-bearer in wonder. "M-M-Marcy," he stumbled over her name.

"The name is Deborah." She cocked her head to the side. "But you already know that, don't you?"

"I can explain," Kraal attempted to speak.

"There is no need to explain." Her words were so cool and

measured. She was now the confident and commanding angel from before, and she wasn't looking at him as if she was happy to see him. "You stole an infant, handed him to the devil himself, then connivingly tricked me into being reborn. Was I an experiment? Let's see how long a light-bearer can be trapped in hell?"

"That wasn't what I thought at all." Kraal took a step forward, but Marcy held up her hand to stop him. "I want what I've always wanted, and that's to be free."

"You don't become free by enslaving others."

Kraal paused before responding. "Marcy—"

"It's Deborah."

"Right. It's strange for me to see you as anything but Marcy… Deborah, I didn't know what I was doing. I saw the infant and couldn't stand the thought of killing him. He was…is…our only chance. I thought if I could convince Drakkon to keep him alive, we could see if the prophecies came true. If you had taken him first, we would have lost our chance."

Deborah watched as Mathilde walked slowly to them. "How are you holding up?"

Mathilde shrugged. She couldn't look Deborah in the eyes.

"I'm so sorry, Mathilde, about everything." There was such sorrow in Deborah's words. "Please give me a chance to make this right."

"You hid your identity in hell. Drakkon said you tricked us so that we'd help you escape."

"I didn't know who I was, and Mathilde, you and I both know that everything about Drakkon is a lie. He only knows hate and destruction. I never wanted to leave you. That's why I'm here. I don't want you to have to go back there."

"I'm scared, Marcy."

"Come with me," Deborah pleaded. She looked from Mathilde to Kraal. "You'll be protected. Then we'll figure out a way to free the Shadows once and for all." To Kraal, she said, "You should have accepted Eli's offer in the first place. You're no good to the Shadows if you're dead."

Kraal had thought the same thing while in the cellar, but he knew what he had to do. "It was fight or flight. I had to get out of there, and my brain wasn't computing anything but to run. And I don't want to save myself at the expense of the other Shadows."

Suddenly, Michael shot straight down from the sky, landing beside Deborah. "Perimeter's clear. We should be able to get them to Eli." He looked at Kraal and Mathilde and said, "There are places we hold as sanctuaries. No evil can inhabit there. You will be safe, but you will also have to be cleansed. The dark seed within you will need to die. This will not be pleasant, but I promise, it will be freeing."

"What of the others?"

"We can't save every Shadow," Michael said.

"Why not?" Kraal and Deborah asked at the same time.

"For several reasons. First of all, there are legions of Shadows in existence. That is a massive undertaking. I'm not saying it isn't doable, but that leads to the next reason. We haven't been released to do such a thing."

"Who releases you? The Nameless One?"

"Drakkon and his legions have never been able to say his name. He is also known as The Most High," Michael said simply. "The Creator of heaven and earth and every realm both in the spiritual and in the physical."

"Drakkon's worst enemy," Mathilde whispered. "He exists?"

"Yes," Deborah and Michael both answered.

"Everything you've been taught is some form of deception," Deborah explained.

"What about the big battle? Is that a lie? I overheard Drakkon talk about talking his rightful place on the throne." Kraal questioned everything he'd ever been told.

"There is a battle, but it will never end with Drakkon being anywhere but hell."

"What about us?" Mathilde asked Deborah. "You and me. Was that a lie too?"

"I feel horrible that you suffered because of our friendship. But I'm here now. Come with me and let me protect you." Deborah went to hug Mathilde, but the Shadow trainee stepped back as if unsure what to do.

Kraal watched Deborah and marveled. Shadows had never felt love or acceptance. That is, until Marcy showed up. Even as a child, she offered hugs and smiles to others in ways that melted the hardened hearts of those around her. Kraal included. Her intense love for him as her mentor shook him because Kraal knew that if the secret ever came out, Drakkon would kill them both. When did he start loving her in return? And was it love he felt? How could he be sure? So many questions, and he desired to live long enough to find out the answers.

He couldn't pinpoint an exact time or moment, but she changed things. If he longed for freedom before her, the longing for freedom now was immeasurably greater.

But what of the others? Shadow existence was mundane at best and torturous at worst. Could he truly leave them?

"Kraal," Deborah spoke to him. "I sense you have questions, and I want you to know that no demon in hell would ever contemplate sacrificing their own freedom and potential happiness for others. There is something different about you. I want you to know that."

"Do you believe that I never meant to hurt you? I've only ever wanted to...have this..." Kraal extended his hands at the early morning sun.

"What I know is that all of your actions had a reason, even if those actions were misguided, deceptive, and questionable."

Kraal turned from the sun to study Deborah. Her long dark hair fell in waves around her. Her face with those piercing blue eyes shone, emanating power. This was the light-bearer he remembered from that fateful day.

"Let's transport them to safety. From there, we can strategize about how to free the rest of the Shadows." Michael waited for Deborah's response.

Kraal felt conflicted. He wanted to be protected and free of Drakkon, but what of the other Shadows? If there was a chance they could be free, shouldn't he at least tell them and give them a chance? Before talking himself out of it, he said, "Take Mathilde. I'm going back." It was the last thing he wanted to do, but what good is freedom while others stay in bondage? He couldn't say the next words out loud. Drakkon couldn't read minds, so this was the safest way to communicate with Deborah.

Would she be able to communicate telepathically?

Yes. The simple word echoed in his thoughts. *I never lost my Shadow abilities.*

Kraal wasted no time. *If Drakkon realizes we're not coming back, he'll torture the Shadows. Many will die. But if I go back, I could lead a resistance.*

Michael offered to pump the well for Mathilde. She nodded vigorously.

Deborah shook her head at Kraal. *It's dangerous. You're linked to me. Drakkon will use you.*

Not if I play this right. If you take Mathilde, I will go back saying that I refused to follow you. I'll vow vengeance.

So, you'll lie.

Kraal frowned. *I'm a product of hell, and I must use hell's tactics to free us. But for the first time, I feel hope. We can do this, Marcy...Deborah.*

What do you plan to do once you get there?

Go to Levea. Many trainees are already on the verge of revolt. Since they travel to the mortal realm together, they provide themselves a certain amount of protection.

Then what? It won't take long for Drakkon to realize that trainees are revolting.

The light-bearers can be at different locations to lead them to safety.

You want light-bearers to hang around? We have assignments. It's not like they can stop what they're doing to help Shadows come to safety. This is massive, Kraal. And the second Drakkon figures it out, every Shadow is dead.

He can't kill us all. We're needed. We're the ones who sway the minds of men. And isn't that what war is all about? Staring death in the face at the thought of what lies beyond it?

"Deborah," Michael approached and gently touched Deborah's arm. "We need to leave."

She nodded, but her gaze never left Kraal. *You'll need to tell them where to go. We will do all we can to protect them, but they must get there first.*

And you remember our meeting place? I'll visit there as often as I can. We can communicate that way. There were several times when Kraal assisted Marcy in sneaking human paraphernalia back to Levea. They would always meet under small bridges in whatever area Marcy had been assigned.

"I hope you know what you're doing," Michael said to Kraal. Then without speaking, he added, *Everything comes down to choice. We can't free those who do not want it.* He looked at a surprised Deborah. *What? I retained my abilities too.*

"Then it's a good thing I didn't say anything bad about you," Deborah teased Michael. They shared a smile. To Kraal, she asked, "Are you sure? You can come with us now."

Kraal understood why she said the words out loud. This was where he needed to establish his plan. He needed to say the words. Is this what he wanted? He paused and took in the view of the sun. He could go with them right now and say goodbye to hell's torment forever. Then he thought of the Shadow trainees. Children, some even younger than Mathilde, born into hell to be slaves. "Go," he said forcefully. "Leave me alone. I may not be able to stop you from taking the girl, but I will tell Drakkon everything. We will get our vengeance."

Michael wasted no time. He grabbed the girl, told her to hold on, and shot straight into the sky. Deborah took one more look at Kraal, a deep frown on her angelic countenance. *Be careful,* she whispered the words to his thoughts before leaving him alone at the well.

Kraal would have laid himself across the ground and let the sun warm him, but his throat was still parched. It'd be difficult to pump and drink at the same time, but his thirst demanded he try. That's when he saw the dilapidated bucket filled to the brim with water. Michael must have found one and filled it while Kraal and Deborah communicated. He knelt beside it and drank heartily.

He felt the shift in atmosphere, but instead of panic, he felt the familiar. He kept drinking.

"I thought they'd never leave," Drakkon said.

"It was hard to part with the trainee, especially knowing how they're going to brainwash her into submission." Kraal pushed himself up and turned to face Drakkon. "But it needed to be done."

Drakkon shrugged. He currently sported his human form. Kraal couldn't decide which was worse: Drakkon masked as a human, or Drakkon unleashed as the red dragon. "I would have killed her."

"We need an inside person. Someone we can manipulate. With Marcy now Deborah, the days of manipulating her are over."

"Are they? Isn't our plan to use the girl to entrap her?"

"We use the girl to lure Tor out of hiding. Tor is the objective."

Drakkon suddenly lashed out, grabbing Kraal's gnarled shirt and pulling him close. "No. I want vengeance on all of them. They all betrayed me, and they all need to suffer." He released Kraal. "Besides, Tor is nothing now. I want the light-bearer. I want her to watch while I torture all she holds dear."

Kraal's skin crawled. He had no doubt Drakkon would torture him when the time came. "What of our deal?"

"What about it?"

"You need my help. Marcy trusts me. Her emotions are her weakness, and I easily manipulate them."

"Which makes you alive. That's the deal."

"You promised—"

"And you promised me Marcy. And what happened? She magically turned into a light-bearer, and together with the other one, they defeated a host of my army!" Drakkon pointed his finger at Kraal, jamming it into his chest. "You get to live. That's the deal. And the second something goes wrong, I'll throw you into outer darkness where you'll beg me to kill you. The abyss would love to have you."

A blue mist appeared, and Drakkon indicated for Kraal to go first. Kraal refused to be afraid. Drakkon could smell it and use it to his advantage. Resisting the urge to admire the sun one more time, Kraal walked through the mist and back into hell.

4

DEBORAH

Deborah stared at her faint reflection through the abbey's kitchen window. Her long, dark hair rested in waves across her shoulders, not a hair out of place. Her blue eyes pierced through the reflection, reminding her of how things had changed. But a twinge of sadness poked at her. "You're not Marcy anymore," she whispered to her reflection.

Since freeing herself from Drakkon's power and becoming Deborah again, she hid the internal struggle she felt. She *still* felt like Marcy, which didn't make sense. She was Deborah long before she was Marcy. Yet, those 20 years in hell changed her. She lived both lives, and both sets of memories were hers.

Her reflection shown like a light had been turned on inside of her. Interestingly, she could see herself in reflections within the mortal realm. She hadn't been able to do that as Deborah. Well, the *pre-Marcy* Deborah, that is. Light-bearers normally did not have reflections. They were spirit beings and could not be seen to the human eye unless they purposefully did so. They called it "expo-sure." But Deborah now could. The human eye could easily see her unless she cloaked herself. Then again, she wasn't an archangel like Michael. She had been a human at one point. Those memories had exploded in her brain when the light-bearer busted through the human shell she had put herself in. But parts of that human shell still remained. "Just another way you're different."

She hadn't shared this with Michael. Her sweet, beloved Michael. He might have been an angelic warrior, but he was hers. She reminded herself of it when thoughts of Tor surfaced. The guilt of his predicament weighed heavily on her. *So many feelings and emotions,* Deborah thought and closed her eyes. And now Mathilde was here, and Kraal was in imminent danger, and Tor was near death. "Deep breaths, girl," she murmured and steadied her breathing.

This uncertainty and the potential volatility of her emotions were two other human traits she still had lingering around. Before she was Marcy, Deborah never struggled with questions or emotions. She was calm, steady, sure.

Should she talk to someone? But who? Michael would listen and understand as best he could, but there were secrets inside of herself that she wasn't comfortable sharing. Too much was going on, and really, what could he do? Her decision to camouflage herself to go into hell and retrieve Tor altered everything. She made a mess of things. She knew it. Michael knew it. Tor knew it. Everyone knew it.

She took one more look at herself, and in exasperation, turned from her reflection. "Enough," she ordered herself. "You are Debo-rah. Now act like it." She moved through the abbey, searching for supplies to help Mathilde. Eli had requested it of her, and Michael agreed that it was a good idea. Deborah didn't argue. She understood what needed to happen, and that it would be dangerous for Mathilde.

She filled a couple canteens with water, grabbed some rags, soap and a wash basin. She also ran up to her old room and selected a change of clothes for Mathilde. Moving outside, she flew into the air, heading quickly to where Eli should be finished cutting the evil seed out of the young Shadow trainee.

Turning her thoughts elsewhere, Deborah slowed mid-air and enjoyed the view. She smiled at the memory of Michael trying to get her to fly by throwing her in the air. Her thoughts turned to Tor. How was he doing? Was he angry with her? Would he ever forgive her for not saving him from being kidnapped? She frowned, knowing that Michael knew where Tor went but agreed to keep it a secret. She understood the reasoning, but it bothered her more than she cared to admit. Sighing, she glanced down at the wash basin and supplies she held onto and descended into the protected forest that surrounded the Irish abbey.

ELI PACED OUTSIDE the cave's entrance. It was the same place that Tor had recuperated before Michael took him and Timothy to wherever they went. "It's not good," he said, without looking up.

Deborah paused before entering. "You weren't successful in extracting and killing the evil seed?"

Eli stopped pacing and turned to Deborah. "She won't release it."

"She won't?" Deborah, pushing aside her distractions, became aware of the underlying darkness. "What is that? That's not Mathilde."

"Whatever it is knows what it's doing. It's pretending to be her."

"It was able to cross the threshold?" Deborah whispered.

Eli nodded. "And I don't understand how or why. Then again, we have never had any creature from hell enter our sanctuaries. Tor was the first. And you...as Marcy..."

"So, where is Mathilde?" Deborah's heart thudded in her chest. Where was her friend? Righteous anger took center stage. "Well, I'm about to find out."

Eli reached for Deborah's arm. In a low tone, he said, "Michael is in there now. We're trying not to let on that we are aware of the ruse. We need information. We also need the other sanctuaries notified. If we've been compromised, any sanctuary could become compromised too."

"I understand that, but we can't allow unrepentant souls to stay here. Allowing darkness only opens the door for more."

"True."

"I have an idea." Deborah walked into the cave and found Mathilde writhing on the small ledge that Eli used as a bed. Deborah was on high alert, sensing immediately that her friend was not the creature on that bed. Deborah identified the same shimmer that Drakkon used when transforming from dragon to human form. "We need to get her out of here," she said to Michael.

"She can't make it out there," Michael said, measuring Deborah with his gaze. She gave a slight nod, indicating that she was aware of the situation. "Drakkon will find her and kill her."

"She won't be alone. I'll go with her and protect her." Deborah noticed Mathilde's writhing paused as if listening to the conversation. "I need to help her figure out why she can't let go of the evil seed."

"She may simply want to hold onto it. She may be too far gone. We may have no other option than to—"

"Mathilde is my friend. I can't abandon her, and she can't stay here. This is the only way."

Michael called out to Eli. He appeared beside us. "I've got to talk to Deborah."

"You two go outside. I'll watch Mathilde."

Deborah left the cave quickly, not liking the darkness she felt. She had escaped hell. She wanted nothing to do with that evil anymore. But she was willing to do whatever was needed to save Mathilde. She didn't stop walking until she stood at the water's edge. It didn't escape her notice that this was the same spot she found Tor after his spiritual rebirth. The same spot they shared their last kiss.

"I'm concerned," Michael said. "I must notify the other sanctuaries. Eli can't leave here. But I'm not sure that I'm okay with you being alone with whatever this impostor is."

"I can handle it," Deborah said. "Whatever it is doesn't stand a chance against me, and you know it."

"That's not why I'm concerned."

"You don't want me making any rash decisions. I get it. I'm not going to, but that thing needs to get out of the sanctuary. How it got it with an unrepentant soul is a mystery." Deborah paused, then admitted, "It feels like everything is broken after my coming back."

"That is not it at all." Michael took Deborah's hands in his. "Please let go of the guilt. Everything happens for a reason. Everything. Which means that this is happening for a reason."

"Yes, and that reason is I made a decision over 20 years ago, unleashing chaos into our realm."

"Maybe you haven't unleashed chaos. Maybe you've walked the path designed for you. This isn't chaos, Deborah. It's divine purpose. You have a big role to play in all of this. I see that now."

"I haven't completely shed the humanity," Deborah admitted. This was the first time she had opened up since her transformation, but Michael didn't act surprised. "My emotions especially are still so volatile. I'm all over the place. One minute I'm weepy, and the next I want to punch someone. It was never this way before."

"Considering your adventure into hell was the first of its kind, we don't know what to expect. It doesn't surprise me that you are different from before, but even that fits into your divine purpose. Don't fight it. Everything happens for a reason, which includes who you are in this moment."

Deborah studied Michael. He was her fierce protector, friend, and betrothed. Her love for him filled her, but something had changed in her. It grieved her because he was so good and kind. "We know what needs to happen," she finally said. "You need to warn the other sanctuaries, and Eli needs to stay here. I need to be the one who delivers this creature back to hell."

"You are not going back there."

"My plan is to get it out of the sanctuary. I'm sure we'll be visited by whoever set this up."

"Drakkon."

"Right. I won't need to go to hell. He'll come to me. He wants to come me. He probably wants to negotiate, and he's using Mathilde as bait."

"What could he possibly negotiate with you? You are a light-bearer. It's not like you could or would cross sides."

"It's not me he wants," she said quietly. "We both know who he wants."

"And he'll want to manipulate Tor by using you."

"Yes. But to find Mathilde, I have no choice but to play his game."

"You do have a choice. We can kill this creature right now and be done with the whole thing. He's already using your compassion and empathy toward Mathilde to get you out of the sanctuary. You don't have to walk right into his trap."

"That's the thing. Yes, I do," Deborah said a little too sharply. "Mathilde is my friend. I realize you don't understand that, but it's true. And this divine purpose that you speak of is connected to her. If it wasn't, I wouldn't feel the way I do."

"I understand a lot more than you think," he said, dropping her hands. "Go then. I won't stop you, but the second there's trouble—and I know there will be—call for me."

Deborah nodded. Michael reached for her, and Deborah stopped thinking long enough to step into his embrace. "I love you," she whispered. "I'm sorry for snapping at you. There's a lot going on in my head right now, but I don't want to ever take it out on you."

"I love you too." He lifted her chin then kissed her. "I'm here for you. Always. Now go show Drakkon who's boss."

5

TOR

Even with his father's incessant sobs, Tor slept hard. When he awoke, it took a moment to remember where he was. He glanced around the small chamber that was no more than a corner of an alcove with large fur blankets, hanging from a rope used as a door. He sat up and noticed he lay on homemade feather bedding stitched within a rough tarp.

"You're awake," Samson pulled back the one side of a hanging blanket. "Arise and wash, and then you can eat a meal."

"Did you make this?" Tor inspected the wood legs and frame of the bed.

"Yes. I like to occupy my time with exercise, both physical and mental. Making things with my hands helps my brain, and it helps the local community."

"The local community? You leave your sanctuary?"

"Yes, my assignment is different than Eli's. I'm here to be called upon at a moment's notice, but my bigger assignment is to protect the locals and help them survive the harsh conditions."

"Humans live on top of this mountain?" Tor shuddered remembering the frigid temps.

"Not this high. But there are villages down the mountain a way."

"And you help them?"

"Yes. Now, go and wash up. You still have blood all over you, and you stink."

"How's Timothy?"

"He's sleeping. It was fitful at first, but he eventually calmed down and has been out ever since." Samson added, "Humanity has no idea what's waiting for them in the spiritual realm. Timothy got to experience the horror of hell through your memories, but it won't break him. If anything, it'll give him a new purpose to help others not meet that fate."

Tor thought of the throngs of human souls entering hell's gates. He would watch, tuning out the wails. The energy now within him shifted, and an unfamiliar scene popped in his head. He was pinned down while a mob of filthy men attacked him. He felt weak and guilty at the same time. A woman stood off in the distance, watching the men attacked, yet she did nothing. Just as quickly as it came, the memory left. "What was that?"

Samson raised an eyebrow. "From your look of confusion and the placement of your hand upon your head, I'm deducing it was a memory. Either mine or Timothy's." Samson tilted his head. "It was one of mine, wasn't it?"

"Were you attacked by a bunch of savages while a woman watched?"

Samson frowned. "Yes, that was me."

Tor made his way to Samson and stepped past the opened blanket. "Who was the woman?"

"You already know. The answer is in there." Samson tapped Tor's head. "I don't talk about her anymore. Now let's get you a change of clothes and some clean water."

As Tor followed Sam, he couldn't shake the woman from the memory. The way her arms were folded across her chest with the slight smile on her face. She was familiar. "Do I know her?"

"I wouldn't be surprised if she hung out in your neck of the woods in the place of torment. She wasn't a good woman, that's for sure."

Tor felt the hurt and betrayal too. "She betrayed you," he said aloud.

Samson grunted then stopped. Tor, still preoccupied by the memory, ran right into him.

Instead of apologizing, Tor took in the mesmerizing view before them. Sunlight from several gaps in the towering rock formation burst through onto crystallized rock, illuminating the entire area. "What is this place?"

"It's a natural stream that goes through the caves all the way down to the deepest valley. It has a lot of uses. The locals at lower elevations use it for drinking, cooking, bathing. I'm usually the only one here, and I'm a spirit-being, so I don't need to wash like I used to. However, this is a good space for you to have some privacy and use the spring."

"Why not? What I mean is why don't you need to wash? I know tons of spirit beings who are disgusting and in need of a good bath."

"They need a bath all right, but not necessarily a mortal one.

Anyway, since you are a mortal, you do need frequent baths. As does Timothy. I'm going to check on him. Oh, and the water is cold. The sun does warm it up in here, but it's still chilly. That big steel pan over the fire is warming some water now."

Tor noticed a fire within a metal, circular contraption. "Is this some type of stove?"

"I guess you could call it that. I needed to build something to warm the water while keeping the fire contained. The natural openings above us helps the smoke to escape. It was the best I could do on short notice. I wasn't exactly expecting you."

"Wait a sec. You just built this?"

"Within the last day or so. You've been sleeping for awhile."

"How did you get the supplies?" Tor thought of Marcy and how she would steal human paraphernalia. He wondered if Samson did something similar.

"I don't steal," he said, "If that's what you're thinking. I have an arrangement with the locals. They help me, and I help them. That's also where the clothing and blankets came from."

"I've tried human clothing before. It doesn't work on me. Burns up in seconds." The memory of Michael irritating Tor, which led to his summoning fire, flashed in his brain. He stood naked in front of Michael and Marcy while they laughed.

Samson began to walk away. "You won't be using fire just yet. When the time comes, you'll have better clothing. For now, it'll work. I'll leave you to it. If Timothy is awake, I'll bring him here."

After Samson left, Tor considered the cold spring or the warm water over the fire. The spring fascinated him. It was a bright blue that sparkled from the sun's hitting of the crystal formations. "Let's see how cold you are." He stripped off his old clothing—oddly it was still the hellish material from his past life. He took one step into the stream and yanked his foot back. It was cold. But the energy within him seemed to encourage him forward, as if it wanted him to go into the stream. He leaned over and glanced in, clearly seeing all the way down. "You want me to jump in?" he asked the energy. He literally felt it push him from the inside. "Fine." Without another thought, he ran and jumped.

The shock of the water's temperature jolted him, but not in the way he anticipated. It was like an amp to the energy within him, making it surge inside to the point it burst from him. He came up out of the water, feeling the power at his fingertips. It was then he realized that he was actually out of the water, flying in the air. He reached up and touched one of the crystals before he descended back into the cold waters. This time it didn't shock him, instead it swirled around him as if it had a mind of its own. Images flooded his brain like a random slide deck. Some from Sam's life, some from Timothy's. It was Timothy's grief that kept replaying. The loss of the child. The hopelessness of watching his wife fade away from the grief. The love and concern that surged through him when he saw Tor for the first time after Drakkon nearly killed him.

Tor surfaced again and took a deep breath. He floated in the water with his eyes closed, concentrating on both men's lives. He truly had captured their memories though he doubted this was even a tiny sliver of their life events. But the loneliness and heartache of his father struck him deeply. The thought of someone loving Tor even when Tor loved nothing and hated everything bewildered him. When he opened his eyes, he saw he had floated beyond the spring and into the stream. The water moved him swiftly past dark parts of caverns; the only light being what now illuminated within him. Did he glow like Sam? Like Michael and Marcy? He didn't dwell on the thought for long because his attention was drawn to the sound of rushing water. He quickly panicked, not desiring to careen down any type of waterfall. He began to swim against the current and wondered if it would be better to get out and walk back by following the water's edge.

Control it. Sam's voice infiltrated Tor's thoughts. He paused long enough to see if Samson had somehow found him. *Control the water, Tor.*

"How?" he asked, the word echoing along the cave's walls. But no response came. "Control it." He had easily controlled fire by summoning it from within himself. But he didn't want to summon the water, he wanted to direct the water. *Stop,* he tried. *Take me back.* He tried speaking to it, "Take me back to the spring." But the water flowed faster downstream. The falls roared in his ear. He swam parallel to the flow and eventually reached a jagged rock along the edge. He gripped it fiercely.

"Here," Samson said, holding a large stick out to him. "Grab hold. I'll pull you out.

"So, you were here?" Tor asked. "Have you been watching me this whole time?"

Samson sighed and shook the stick. "Take hold before I change my mind and let you crash against the rocks."

Tor reached for the stick and grabbed it with one hand. The other had slipped off the rock, making him twist and turn in the water. He finally got both hands secured around it, and Samson pulled him out without so much as breaking a sweat. The words thank you sat on his tongue, but they were still so foreign to him. "I'm naked," he finally said.

Samson handed him one of the blankets. He took it and wrapped it around himself.

"What are you doing here?"

"Saving your life apparently."

"How did you know where I was?"

"You already know the answer. Eli and I may have different assignments, but we have similar abilities. My presence infiltrates these caves. If you ever need me, I'll know it. If you call out to me, I'll hear you."

"Do you leave the caves when helping the locals?"

"Yes."

"You leave your sanctuary?"

"Yes."

"Are you protected?"

"Yes. Not in the same way as when I'm in here, but I can't be killed again if that's what you're asking."

"Technically, you killed yourself," Tor said, recalling the memory of Samson pushing the pillars in such a way the roof caved in on him and everyone in it.

"Ah, you have retrieved my memories."

"It's strange. Part of your memories I can see vividly, and others I can only hear."

"That would be when they plucked my eyes out."

"Right. That memory is pretty vivid. But hey, look on the bright side, you've got your eyes now."

"On this side of the realms, yes, but when I go to the locals, they see my physical characteristics much like you did when you first arrived. How about we hold off on the questions, until you have clothes on and some food in your stomach?"

Tor's stomach rumbled. "Sounds good. How far did I float?"

"So much for holding off on questions, huh?" Samson motioned for Tor to follow, then he began heading in the direction Tor traveled from. "You floated far. I left you hours ago."

"Hours? It felt like minutes. Then again, my internal clock has been off since being in the mortal realm."

"Timothy has already bathed and dressed and is finishing his meal."

"Did he experience what I experienced?" Tor followed Samson through tunnels and passageways with parts at a steep angle. Not that it bothered Tor. He felt completely like himself sans his abilities. And even then, he wondered if he was getting them back. "The water seemed alive and responsive to me. And it shocked the energy in me and woke it up or something. I haven't felt this good since...I don't remember ever feeling like this."

"Timothy chose the warm water for his bath. You chose the cold spring, which is interesting. I didn't think you'd jump in."

"It pushed me. Whatever it is that's inside me now. It wanted me in the water."

Samson stopped walking and studied Tor with sudden fascination and maybe some appreciation too. "That's interesting. You willingly baptized yourself in holy water."

"I did what?"

Samson continued walking, so Tor moved along with him. This time he easily kept his pace. "You baptized yourself in very special waters. Let's just say that. I had to give you a choice to see if you were responsive yet to the light now residing in you."

"It's light? That energy I feel? Do you have the same thing?"

"Yes, it's divine light. It has accepted you and found you worthy, which is a great gift. Normally, it happens to human souls who have walked a worthy life while in the mortal realm. But you are still alive, which makes this unique."

"And if I had chosen the warm bath?"

Samson shrugged. "Then you would have chosen what your flesh wanted, which most humans would do, like Timothy. Nothing wrong with that. I thought that's what you would have picked. I didn't know how much time it would take for you to truly be in tune with the light."

"Will Timothy choose the holy water at some point?"

"I don't know. He doesn't have the same calling as you have. Your purposes are intertwined yet different." Samson stopped again. "I must be honest. I'm not sure about any of this. This is new to me. Michael just showed up and handed me a human anomaly to train. It has never happened. At least not in my knowledge. And then it went from one human to two humans. I wasn't expecting you, but I understood Michael's rationale to train you. You are to fulfill the prophecy of helping protect mankind from Drakkon's war. But Timothy? I definitely wasn't expecting him. There's no prophecy about him, and he doesn't have any special giftings."

"I was surprised you let him stay. I'm conflicted about him. He's my father, but he's a stranger."

Samson motioned for them to keep moving. "His love for you is fierce, and I could not rip that apart. He reminds me in some ways of my own father."

"Your father's in your memories. He and your mother were so small compared to your size."

"He worked tirelessly to protect me. Mostly from myself. I was my biggest enemy. I realized it too late."

There was melancholy in Sam's words, so Tor didn't pursue the topic. Tor looked behind him. They had been walking the passageways and climbing steps for some time. "My word. Did I float down the entire mountain?"

"You wish." Samson snorted. "This mountain is massive, and my sanctuary doesn't even span a quarter of it. But you floated all the way to the waterfall, which is quite a hike when you're walking."

"By the time we get back, I'm going to need another bath."

The passageway opened into a living area with natural sunlight peeking through a variety of openings above them. A large dining table and benches surrounding it sat in the center. Another stove-like contraption was in the corner of the area and numerous shelves lined the rest of the walls. Timothy sat at the table with a young woman. Both acted startled when Samson and Tor approached them.

Timothy's attention focused on Tor. "Son."

"Hello," Tor said, suddenly aware of how naked he was underneath the blanket. He also noticed the dark circles under Timothy's eyes not there before. "I hope you're better."

"Samson and Lin have been helping me." He pointed at the young lady standing beside him.

She bowed low, then stood rigid straight with her eyes still cast downward. She was petite with long raven hair and pale skin with a scattering of freckles across her nose. "I am Lin," she spoke in English with a heavy accent.

Tor glanced at Samson who smiled at the girl. When he saw Tor waiting for an explanation, he said, "Lin is my daughter. Lin, this is Tor, and I see that you've met Timothy."

"Yes, he enjoyed our lamb stew." She looked over at Samson and smiled in return. She had a beautiful smile.

Tor coughed and looked away. He was not in any state to admire her beauty. "I need to change."

Samson nodded, then pointed forward. "Keep in the same direction, and you'll enter the bathing area. It's straight shot and not far at all. We'll be in here waiting for you."

Lin made eye contact with Tor and bowed again.

"Got to go," he said gruffly. He left the chamber, moving fast. Too much had happened, and he didn't need or desire any more complicated, human emotions. What he wanted was to tap into whatever this energy was. If it was divine light, and it approved of him, he wanted to make sure he stayed worthy. Because what he wanted more than anything was to have his power back. He was smart enough to know that all his former training took place in hell, but this was a fresh start. It was a chance to tap into something compelling and good. Tor might not know what that looked like or where it would lead him, but he was more than ready.

Even the energy inside of him pulsed in excitement.

6
KRAAL

He stepped through the blue mist and into Levea, where all Shadow trainees camped. Drakkon was close behind him. Kraal found it eerily quiet. It was the space where Marcy had lived with her group of trainees, but now there was no noise, nothing. Even if the older trainees had left for their nightly assignment, the young Shadow trainees would still be here. When he turned around, he saw Drakkon watching him. "Where is everyone?" He tried to sound nonchalant and hoped his voice didn't betray him.

"They're gone. All of them."

"Where?" Kraal tried to swallow, but a big lump had formed in his throat.

"Disintegrated, for the most part. I threw a couple Rakye's way, but the Guardians took care of the rest."

Kraal knew not to show emotion. It was useless, but there was something inside that felt an awful lot like grief. "You killed them? Every trainee, or just the ones in Marcy's group?"

"All of them. We don't need them anymore. We have more than enough Elder Shadows to sway the ways of men. Besides, mankind is so wicked on their own, we're getting to the point where we don't need the Elder Shadows either."

Kraal felt fear grip him. He had made a big mistake. He could have gone with Michael and Deborah, but he walked right back into hell and to the prince of darkness himself. What did he think he could do? Stop Drakkon and the host of demons in hell? All of which had power to kill him. And now he would die here. For nothing. "So, this is where I die."

"That's up to you," Drakkon said with a smirk on his face. He clearly enjoyed this.

"I'm listening."

"Bring me Tor."

"I don't know where he is."

"Find him, and then bring him to me. You did it once. You can do it again. This next part is non-negotiable: he must come willingly. He cannot be kidnapped, bribed or lied to outright, or we'll have another catastrophe on our hands. Your rash actions when Tor was an infant has caused mass casualties to my numbers."

"It wasn't supposed to. I was simply trying to give hell the advantage."

"Well, you didn't. You brought two light-bearers into our midst, and together, they destroyed thousands of my dark soldiers."

"I didn't know Marcy would explode like that! I didn't know she'd reject the signing of the book!" Kraal tried to plead his case even though it was hopeless.

You didn't know," Drakkon said mockingly. "You stupid, pathetic Shadow. That's why your entire lot is nothing but slaves.

You do what you're told! That's it. I want to peel your skin in layers and watch you squirm in pain, but luckily for you, I still find you marginally useful. Bring me Tor, and make sure he comes willingly. By doing so, he exercises free will, and there is nothing the light-bearers can do about it. Do this, and you will live."

"If he chooses to come to you, can't he also choose to leave?"

"If he's still alive, yes, but I'm going to torture and kill him. It'll be even more satisfying if Marcy is there to watch. If he's dead, she'll be destroyed. The grief and guilt she'll feel will weaken her. Then the light-bearers can't use him to help save humanity because they'll be too busy trying to save their precious light-bearer. And I'll be free and clear to unleash my destruction on the mortal realm."

"It sounds like a good plan," Kraal said, trying his best to preserve his life until he can get help.

"Of course, it is. Tor is the missing piece. It would have been handy keeping Marcy with us, but who knew that she was a light-bearer herself?" Drakkon tilted his head and glared at Kraal.

"I thought keeping her identity hidden would better help our cause!"

"You have many mistakes against you," Drakkon hissed out the words through clenched teeth. "You kidnapped a human child, and you helped rebirth a light-bearer into my kingdom! The only reason you are still alive is because you have a relationship with these individuals. Only you can reach them in a way that'll turn this around in my favor."

"If I accomplish this, will you grant me my freedom?"

Drakkon moved so fast, Kraal didn't have time to think. He grabbed the Shadow by the throat, shifting his persona into that of the red dragon. His hand turned into talons, and they were dangerously close to Kraal's vital veins. "You are mine, slave. You will always be mine."

"Then just kill me now. I'd rather be dead than be your slave."

Drakkon threw him in the air and down the waterfall. This waterfall was torture because it was an illusion. There was no water in hell. Just the same the drop was steep, and Kraal freefell until he landed beside the fiery pit. The souls wailed and screamed from within it. Drakkon's cage was at the ready. At first, Kraal thought Drakkon would throw him in one, until he saw that in several cages were the Shadow trainees of Marcy's unit. Arec, one of Marcy's friends, noticed Kraal and began to plead. "Help us. He's killing us off one by one." He quieted as Drakkon approached them.

"Do I need to make room in one of the cages?" Drakkon asked Kraal. "They were a lot more of the slaves, but it's become a fun game. It's their screams as they're thrown into the fire that does it for me."

The trainees cowered together in the cages, and Kraal felt another emotion stir within him: anger. Now *that* was an emotion he was used to. He thought of Mathilde and Marcy—now Deborah —and the relief in knowing they were not trapped here surprised him. He knew what he had to do. He had to find Tor. The last thing he wanted was to double-cross him or the light-bearers, but if the prophecy was true, Tor was the answer. "We have a deal. I'll find Tor and bring him here."

"It must be willingly."

"And it will be."

Drakkon extended the blue mist. "I know that Tor is in a light-bearer sanctuary in the Himalayan mountains. We tracked Michael's flight to that point. They went into the storm clouds and never left. Michael can disguise his travel when he's alone, but not when carrying a human. That means Tor is there. Unfortunately, I don't know the exact location of most of these sanctuaries, which means you still have a lot of ground to cover."

"A little bit of an understatement since the Himalayan mountain range covers thousands of miles and crosses several countries."

"Then get started." Drakkon grabbed Kraal's arm and clasped a shackle around his wrist. He felt the searing pain immediately from the poison. "This will slowly kill you. If I don't see Tor within five mortal days, you will be dead. If you bring him to me by then, I will take this off your wrist and let you live."

Kraal could barely think straight with the poison already working. But Drakkon didn't wait for him to speak. Instead, he shoved Kraal through the blue mist and into the mortal realm. Kraal found himself right back next to the well. He dropped to his knees, and for a moment, allowed himself to deal with the agonizing weight of what he had to do. Any decision resulted in his death and the Shadows losing. If he brought Tor to Drakkon? Drakkon would use the gifted human anomaly to hurt Marcy and wage war against mankind, and the Shadows would forever be slaves. If he resisted, Drakkon would kill him, and all the Shadows would die or be in grave danger. If he had the capability to cry, he would because the despair was too much. "I only want to be free," he whispered in anguish. Drakkon or his minions would probably be listening, but Kraal no longer cared. Because in any scenario, he either ended up dead or a slave for eternity.

He stayed there, out in the open, until the sun set, and the darkness descended. He felt Michael's presence before he saw him. Kraal contemplated telling him everything. But would this light-bearer care? Michael blamed Kraal for taking Marcy—Deborah—from him all those years ago.

"I take it things did not go as planned," Michael said as he approached.

Kraal held up his one arm, displaying the poisonous shackle. "I'll be dead in a few days."

"What's the catch? Knowing Drakkon, there's some sinister plot to all of this."

Kraal looked away.

"He wants Deborah?" Michael paused then the realization illuminated his features. "He wants Tor."

Kraal nodded. "He wants both. If he kills Tor, then Marcy suffers."

"And, let me guess, you have to bring him to Drakkon before the poison in that shackle kills you."

Kraal nodded again.

"Why didn't you just come with us?"

"I don't know," Kraal said honestly. Telling the truth, especially in a way that wasn't meant to be used in manipulation, felt foreign to Kraal. He was good at lying, manipulating the truth, and any other form of deviance. But purposeful truth-telling was considered a weakness in hell because it exposed vulnerabilities. But lying to Michael, who could probably read him anyway, seemed futile. "I've felt torn since first seeing the baby all those years ago. Something inside me changed or shifted. I don't know. I never had a reason to hope, but that moment opened my eyes to the possibility of being free. I never knew how much I wanted freedom until seeing Tor as an infant and hearing the prophecy of the human anomaly. My eyes had been deceived my entire miserable existence." Kraal turned to

Michael and met his gaze. He could never make eye contact with a human. If a mortal stared into his eyes, they'd be staring into the darkest abyss. But light-bearers were different. They weren't afraid of the abyss. Their master had already defeated it. "I know you blame me for what happened to Marcy...*Deborah*."

"You are responsible for the kidnapping of the human child. Everything else, Deborah decided to do voluntarily. And I understand. Being in hell all those years, waiting for the moment to rescue Deborah and Tor, watching as the Guardians brutalized the Shadow trainees, it was all I could do to stay in disguise."

"The Shadows still bear the brunt of Drakkon's wrath. Most of the trainees are killed already. He keeps the ones in Marcy's group in cages. He's killing them off one by one." Kraal took a breath, his throat burning. He needed water.

"Here," Michael said, pumping the well. "Take a drink."

With Michael's strength, it didn't take long for water to gush out of the spigot. Kraal thirstily drank. When he had his fill, he asked, "How's Mathilde?"

"She's getting the help she needs. That's where Deborah is. She didn't want to leave, so she sent me to bring you to her. Interestingly, she's connected with you. She found you and Mathilde easily, and she immediately sensed when you were back in the mortal realm. Somehow being a Shadow made her family to all of you."

"I can't sense her when she's far away, then again, I'm not a light-bearer. But I did feel the shift in the atmosphere when she and you were close." Kraal wiped his mouth and pushed himself off the ground. He placed a hand on his stomach as the nausea rolled. "I don't know what to do. If I bring Tor to Drakkon, he's dead, and I'm a slave forever. If I don't, this poison will kill me."

"Tor can't go back," Michael said.

"He's the only chance we have of being free. That's why I stole him in the first place. The prophecy said that whatever side he was fighting on would win."

"If Drakkon kills him, then what?"

Kraal thought about it. "In Drakkon's mind, if Tor is dead, then mankind has no hope of winning. He'd rather take him out of the equation. Then again, he's seeing red right now and vowing vengeance. That trumps everything else."

"How do you plan to capture Tor? He may lack his powers, but he *is* savvy to hell's manipulative ways. Not to mention, he's under protection in one of our hidden sanctuaries."

"And it gets even better," Kraal added with sarcasm. "He needs to come willingly. It won't work if it isn't an act of free will."

"And if you can't get to him?"

"You already know the answer to that." Kraal held up his shackled wrist.

Michael reached out and took Kraal's wrist in his large hand. "You know you're descended from humans, right?"

"Partly. Humans mated with hell's soldiers, but that was ions ago."

"Actually, you are entirely human, which is why you can still mate with each other and produce infants. It is also why you connect more with each other than the demons, and it is also why you can die, and all the other creatures of hell cannot. At least not in the same way as you and other Shadows."

"Last I checked, I still had black orbs for eyes, can move through the shadows in seconds, and can manipulate human thought from a hundred yards away. Not exactly the next-door neighbor mortals would want."

Michael glanced around, then said, "Let's get going. I'll take you to Eli and see what can be done. But as you stated before, there are eyes and ears everywhere. But Kraal, you need to understand one important piece of information."

"What?"

"You're not alone in this fight. You never have been."

"It hasn't felt that way." Kraal decided to communicate the next piece privately. *Are we going to the Irish Abbey? I remember how to get there. It's not far from here.*

Before Kraal understood what was happening, Michael picked him up and flew vertically into the air. "This is even faster."

7

TOR

Tor sat cross-legged in front of the fire staring into Sam's contraption. He'd been sitting there coaxing himself to give it a try. He wasn't necessarily afraid of fire. If anything, he desired it to be a part of him like it was before. But he also knew he was human and was currently dressed in human clothing. He told himself to stick his hand in it and see what happened. But human skin didn't repel fire.

"Are you finding the fire fascinating?" Timothy approached Tor from behind, then sat beside him in front of the fire.

"I'm trying to talk myself into sticking my hand in it."

"Why would you want to do that?"

"I used to control it. I was hoping that power had come back to me. I won't know unless I try."

"Of course. You were—are—quite powerful."

Tor turned to his father who now had dark circles under his

eyes. "I did that to you." He pointed to the dark circles. "I didn't understand that you would fully experience everything about my past. If I had known, I wouldn't have gone through with it. I'd have sent you packing."

"And I would have insisted on staying. You are my son. I know that feels foreign to you, but now that I know you're alive, I'm going to fight to protect you. I'm also going to fight to be with you. So there."

An unexpected emotion filled Tor. He felt *wanted*. He had never felt that before. "That doesn't make any sense."

Tor turned his attention to the fire. Timothy took his hand. Tor nearly yanked his hand away, but he reminded himself that this man was his father and for the last two decades thought his only son was dead. "I'm so sorry." Timothy's words were filled with sorrow. "I'm so sorry that you went through the horrors of hell. We humans truly have no idea what awaits us."

"You saw everything?"

"No. Samson told me that the divine energy inside of you protected me from the worst of it. I merely saw a glimpse into your past."

"Really? You were so...affected by it. What did you see?"

"I saw little pieces of scenes; they were moving so fast through my brain. You, as a little boy, in a cage over flames, you in complete darkness, screaming for help. You being trained by these hideous creatures. They were trying to rip you apart."

"Luckily, I was a fast learner," Tor said quietly. Those moments from his past now haunted his thoughts. He learned at a young age not to dwell on them for too long because it only fed the despair. "It was in the cage that I first learned I controlled fire. It was in the dark pit that I learned I could manipulate the realms. I was able to conjure up a blue mist, and I walked right out. When Drakkon found out, he was so angry yet also impressed. I found out that keeping him impressed kept the abuse at bay, so I worked hard to impress him. Soon, I was his right-hand man."

"Yeah, I saw that too. I saw the storms you created, and the masses of people in danger."

"I killed a lot of them," Tor admitted. "It brought Drakkon such joy, if you can even call it that. He would be deliriously happy at the throngs of humanity entering hell."

"I also saw the ones you saved. When no one was looking, I saw through your eyes, the crying children you'd protect."

"I didn't want children suffering my fate," Tor whispered. "Most of the children don't go to hell, but still, the thought of separating them from their parents was too much for me." The two of them watched the fire, both lost in their thoughts. A question sat on Tor's tongue, but he felt awkward asking it. Eventually, he looked over at Timothy and asked, "What was she like? My mother?"

"She was beautiful. Just as beautiful on the inside as she was on the outside. She loved children and couldn't wait until we had our own. That's how we filled our time in the years before you. We helped build orphanages around the world. The children adored her." Timothy stared off into the distance, a faint smile on his lips. It was the first time Tor observed him smile since after they clasped hands.

"I was your only child?"

"We had several miscarriages. Each time, she would try to

encourage me. She'd say, 'We'll keep trying, and soon, God will grant us our desires.' Then she'd go pour herself into the lives of the children around us."

"God…" Tor whispered the word. In hell, he'd have been severely punished for just the mention of Drakkon's most-hated enemy. But to hear Timothy talk of the divine-being felt as if they were talking about family. It confused Tor. "Could the divine-being not grant you children? Is that not his gifting?"

"His gifting?" Timothy studied Tor, a full grin spreading across his countenance. "I've never heard of God having a gifting. He *is* the gift. It was Him that gave you exactly what you needed to escape those situations. The gift of fire, the gift of transporting realms, the gift of controlling the atmosphere. Have you never stopped to consider it? Every time, you were given a way out."

"Why would he do that?" Tor became more confused. "I killed people with those gifts. I thought the Nameless One loved humans. They are his pets or something like that. Why would he give me gifts to hurt those he loves?"

"I don't have all the answers, but I know that He was looking out for you. It brings me much-needed peace."

Tor stared at his father with some serious misgivings. How can Timothy act so blindly accepting? "I still have questions, but if you have some peace, then I'm glad for it. As for my mother, I wish I could have met her."

"She was so excited for you." Timothy smiled sadly. "It took a lot from us when you went missing. We searched and searched. The hospital security cameras showed nothing. It was like you vanished into thin air. It was too much for her. The miscarriages and then your disappearance, it all weighed heavily on her. And that's not blaming you at all. You were merely an infant."

"It was Kraal," Tor said with a frown. "He kidnapped me. Marcy was supposed to protect me, and she was too late."

"Don't." Timothy released Tor's hand and rested his own hand on Tor's shoulder. "Don't become bitter. We can't change the past."

"Don't become bitter? Kraal robbed me of a normal life! He robbed me of my parents! And Marcy failed, and I suffered the consequence. But not her. She's back to being Deborah the light-bearer. Everything about my life sucked, and if God was so intent on providing me a way out of situations, why did he put me in hell to begin with?" Tor stood up fast, needing to do something to work off his anger.

"Tor." Timothy pointed at Tor's hand. When Tor glanced down, he saw the fire from the contraption, reaching out and licking his fingers.

Tor lifted his hand and stared at the fire at his fingertips. He played with it and easily held it in his palm.

"It doesn't even burn you." Timothy watched as Tor created another fireball in his other hand. Still, there was trepidation in his voice when he added, "Be careful with that."

Tor laughed as he threw the fire balls from one hand to another. He closed his eyes, inhaled deeply, and immediately felt the fire within himself. He pushed it out, exploding around him. Until he heard Timothy cry out in terror.

He turned quickly and saw Timothy shrinking back toward the cold spring of water. The sheer horror on his father's face startled Tor back into reality. "It's okay," he said, stepping toward his father. "I can control it."

Timothy had nowhere left to go, so he fell in, sputtering as he came out.

"What are you doing?" Samson roared. Without so much as touching Tor, he somehow lifted him up and threw him into the water.

Tor came back up, coughing. "There was no need to do that."

Samson helped Timothy out of the water and wrapped another blanket around his shoulders.

Tor called out to his father. "I wasn't going to hurt you. I would never—" He stopped talking as he stepped out of the water and sighed. He was naked. "I hate human clothes."

By the time Samson came back, Tor had already wrapped the same blanket from before around his waist. "What was that?" Samson asked.

Tor smiled. "I've got my power back. Oh, and I need my other clothes. They don't disintegrate. Kind of important unless I'm supposed to walk around naked all the time."

"You're not an agent of hell anymore, Tor. The goal is not for you to retain the powers from your past, but to train and use your powers for good. They'll be transformed."

"I can use fire for good."

"What I saw was a demon clothed in fire. That's what I walked in on. Timothy was terrified. Your eyes had flames in them. That isn't light."

Tor closed his eyes for a moment and tried to find the light energy from before. But it was eerily quiet. "Where'd it go?"

"You can only serve one master. The divine light will not interfere with your decisions, and that decision was to fall back into dark power. How were you able to manipulate the flame?"

"It just happened. Timothy and I were talking, and I stood up fast. He told me to look at my hand, and the fire from in your home-made furnace or stove or whatever it is reached out to me."

"What made you stand up so quickly? What was the conversation?"

"Why does it matter?"

"Because it does."

"We were talking about my mother." Tor paused as he remembered. "I was angry," he said more to himself. "Timothy warned me not to become bitter, but I got up off the ground because I was mad and wanted to walk it off."

"The fire feeds off your anger."

The realization hit Tor, and he brought his hands up, staring at them intently. "For all these years, I've controlled fire because I've been angry?"

"It seems that way."

"How was I able to access realms and to transport myself?"

"I don't have all the answers, but I'm starting to think that it too feeds off of some negative emotion."

Tor dropped his hands. "Let me get this straight. Without negative emotions, I will be powerless?"

"No, you are definitely powerful. The key is to be patient and let me train you. Accessing the spirit realm means there are two sides. You've been trained on one side. In order to train on the other side, you can't feed negativity. Darkness and light—"

"Yes, I know. Darkness and light cannot mix. I get it. Eli told me a million times, and you're looking to break the record."

"That's an exaggeration. I'm sure he did *not* tell you a million times, but we remind you of it because it's true."

"Can I *please* have some type of clothing that doesn't disintegrate?"

"Did you just say please?"

"Maybe." Tor thought a moment. "I think I did. So, does that mean I can get better clothes?"

"No, but I am impressed that you're using some manners. Use some with your father and go apologize."

"Get me better clothes, and I will."

"Are you trying to manipulate me to do your will? Because you know who does that? Drakkon and his legions. You know who does *not* do that? Us."

"Newsflash: I was raised by Drakkon. It's not a light switch I can turn off."

"We are going to first train in other weapons. I'm asking you to please not access fire again. Doing so connects you with your dark past, and light cannot mix—"

"With darkness," Tor finished for him. He rolled his eyes. "Yeah, yeah, yeah, I know. Is that why the energy left? I can't feel it anymore."

"Here's an important lesson. One I had to learn too. We all serve a master."

"I want to serve no one. I'm done serving masters."

"It's not open for discussion."

"No need to be a jerk about it." Tor nearly created a fireball. *Let's see how fast he could dodge one*, he thought with a smirk.

"All I'm saying is we don't make the rules. But know this. When you choose to operate in darkness, you have chosen your master. When you choose to operate in the light, you have chosen your master."

"So, by choosing to rekindle the fire within me, I chose darkness?"

"Sort of, yes. Which is why you are not connected with the light inside of you. When you choose to serve darkness, the light will step back. When you choose to serve the light, or really, who the light represents, the darkness must flee."

"Which is why you don't want me to play with fire right now? Admit it, you wouldn't stand a chance," Tor said it teasingly, or at least, he tried to, but it came out more like a taunt.

Samson took a step closer. "Oh Tor, are you really going to challenge me to a fight? Have you not witnessed my memories? I killed a thousand men with the jawbone of a donkey. I barely broke a sweat."

Tor recalled that memory from Samson's life. Tor didn't want to back down. He still itched to fight, but he didn't know if he had any other ability. He would need to lay low for a while longer. "Will I ever be able to control fire again? Will I be able to control it in such a way that I don't scare people?"

"Fire is dangerous because its purpose is often meant to destroy. But there is such a thing as a holy fire. As you learn and train, hopefully, you will learn to control in it in that way."

"Holy fire," Tor repeated, liking the sound of it. He felt the small buzz of energy inside. It was still there. He sighed in relief. Because even though he thrilled at the thought of having his powers back, none of that felt the way the light did when it surged through him. But if he could have light and fire? He'd be unstoppable. "I'm ready to train."

"Good. The first step is to go apologize to your father."

Tor pressed his lips together, defiance brewing. "I don't see the point in that. He'll be fine. I wasn't going to hurt him."

"Go apologize." Samson left Tor, closing the discussion.

Tor glanced down at the towel wrapped around his waist. Calling out, he asked, "Can I get some clothes?"

8

KRAAL

"You can't enter." Eli frowned as he stared at Kraal's wrist. Since Eli was a Guardian over this light-bearer sanctuary, he could not leave the forest. So, Kraal stood on one side of the trees, and Eli on the other. "Drakkon has claimed you."

Kraal lifted his hand and inspected the shackle. It appeared as nothing more than an old, rusty wrist band, but there was a thin, red line through it that pulsated rhythmically. "A slow and painful death, right?"

"Not necessarily."

Kraal snapped his head up, surprised by Eli's answer. "Are you sure? It looks like it's final to me."

"You are still human, which means that free-will applies to you. Every single Shadow could walk right out of hell if they wanted to. That's what is sad about the whole thing. None of you have to stay."

Kraal laughed humorlessly. "You've obviously never witnessed a Shadow being turned to ash. Trust me, if we could leave, we would

69

have. *I* would have. A long time ago. And this whole situation with Tor would have never happened."

"You believe a lie," Eli said.

"It's not a lie. Go ask Mathilde if her arm got burned off. Go ask the Shadow trainees in a cage over the lake of fire as we speak if it's a lie." Kraal felt himself getting worked up. Being in the mortal realm always brought more emotions with it. "Or just ask me who has a poisonous shackle around his wrist."

"What I'm saying is *you* believe *yourself* to be a slave. You were born into it. Those Shadows ahead of you told you it was so. You watched as monsters in hell abused and burned other Shadows around you. It was an easy lie to believe. Because of millennia of this treatment, Shadows took their place right where Drakkon wanted them. Under his control."

All Kraal could do was shake his head. "You don't know what you're talking about."

"Yes, he does." Michael approached from behind Eli. He had left them to go check on Mathilde per Kraal's request. "You were all a part of Drakkon's experiment to pervert the Master's plan. He wanted his own human race, but Drakkon is not, nor will he ever be, a creator. He is merely an imitator. Thus, when his generals mated with human women, they brought many of the children to hell. They didn't know what would happen. They didn't expect how powerful you would be but also how fragile."

"Because we stayed human?"

"Yes, spirit beings in mortal shells. That meant you could be controlled by fear."

"They figured out they could kill us."

"Yes, but they wanted your abilities to control the shadows

because the shadows could be linked to human consciousness. Thus, they placed you under their thumb. No one asked questions. Everyone did what they were told."

"Shadows are extremely gifted," Eli added. "You can manipulate human thoughts?"

"Yes, many of us can. We start by training the young to tap into humans while they're sleeping. Mortals are mostly harmless during slumber, and trainees can practice the skill. The older they get, some show more talent than others. Some will not do much more than that, and those are the expendable ones. They die quickly."

Eli glanced at Michael and raised his eyebrows.

"We technically can't read minds."

"So, you can't read my thoughts right now?"

"No. I can communicate my thoughts to mortals if I'm in proximity. There are times when I can hear the thoughts of others, but only if they are aware of me and sending the thought my way."

"He can't read minds," Michael said to Eli. "Only God is omniscient."

"Which is why I asked the question. I was trying to fully understand these Shadows' capabilities." To Kraal, Eli said, "It explains why Drakkon has claimed you. It sounds as if you are a powerful Shadow with abilities that most do not possess."

"I can't be that powerful since he's put a death sentence on me."

"You did it once," Michael said. "You brought Tor to him years ago. Drakkon's betting that you'll do it again."

"Unfortunately, until that thing comes off of you, I can't let you enter."

Kraal closed his eyes and repeated in his head, *You are not a slave. You are not a slave.* When he opened his eyes, the shackle was still there, although the red line slightly dimmed. Or he thought it had. "Did you see that?"

"Yes," Eli said. Michael nodded.

Careful, Michael projected his thoughts to Kraal. *Drakkon cannot know that you are doing this. He has too much to lose for you and other Shadows to walk free.*

Kraal nodded in understanding. Making sure there was a bite to his words, he said, "Listen, I don't have time for either of you to get into my head. Hope is futile, and it gets us killed. I'm here for Tor."

Eli looked from Tor to Michael, eyebrows raised. "If you think we would ever tell you, then the poison must be making you delirious."

"I already know which mountain range. It's only a matter of time until I find him."

"But will you have enough time is the question," Michael asked.

Kraal felt sick. There was so much to do, and the last thing he needed was the mortal realm messing with him. He placed a hand on his stomach, and then turned quickly to not wretch in front of them. The sickness repeated. Suddenly, he felt the shift in the atmosphere. Whatever it was had to be powerful, and he spun around, searching for who it could be. Michael and Eli weren't looking at Kraal. Instead, they seemed to silently communicate with each other. To Michael, Kraal asked, "What is it? I felt it. What light-bearer is more powerful than you?" Kraal could still feel it. He no longer felt sick. In a weird way, he felt calm and attuned to his surroundings.

"No light-bearer is more powerful than Michael," Eli answered. "That wasn't a light-bearer."

Michael looked to Kraal and projected his thoughts. *Go to the northernmost point of the Himalayan mountains. There is a village with a tree within it whose leaves will be entirely gold. Wait there.*

Kraal looked from Michael to Eli. *Why are you helping me?*

Because he told me to help. Whatever you were sent to do needs to happen.

Chills shot up Kraal's spine. *The Nameless One? He's helping me?*

Michael didn't answer the questions, but he pointed to the shackle. *Keep working on changing your thoughts about slavery but keep it to yourself. You have a lot more power than you realize.*

Kraal watched as Michael and Eli disappeared into the forest. There was so much to process, but first, he needed to get moving. The journey would be long even with travelling in shadows.

He didn't travel far before being snatched through a blue mist. He landed hard, smacking his head on hell's ground. He was in Drakkon's throne room surrounded by demons and Guardians. One particular Guardian, Moshi, glowered over him. Kraal hated Guardians. They were behemoths in size with war scars dating back centuries. But they were the gatekeepers to the mortal realm and Shadows couldn't travel back and forth without them.

"Bring him to me," Drakkon said.

Moshi grabbed Kraal by the neck, lifted him up, and carried him to the throne. He dropped him at Drakkon's feet.

"Did you get any information? I figured if you were alone, those horrible light-bearers would try to help. They just can't stop themselves. And don't lie to me. You were travelling quite fast, as if you knew where you were going."

"Yes, I have information, and I'm wasting time." Kraal rubbed his head which currently sprouted a large goose egg. He hated the frailty of his humanity.

"What did you learn?"

Kraal couldn't give him all the information, but he would need to give him something. "There's a village in the northern Himalayans that light-bearers frequent. There's a good chance one of their sanctuaries is close by. My goal is to find it."

Drakkon nodded. "Yes, this is valuable information. Moshi will be with you from this point on. For travel purposes, of course. Oh, and to kill you should you try anything."

Moshi reached for Kraal, but this time, Kraal anticipated it and stepped aside. "Keep your hands off me." To Drakkon, he said, "I don't need a babysitter. I have this. Remember?" He held up his shackled hand.

Drakkon stared at Kraal a moment, slowly moved toward him, then slapped him so hard, his ears rang. Kraal lost his balance and fell to the ground. Immediately, he felt the blow of Drakkon's kick to his stomach. "Do you forget your place?" he seethed. "You don't tell me what to do. Ever."

The demons surrounding them chanted excitedly. They anticipated the shedding of Shadow blood.

"Maybe I send Moshi to retrieve Tor. Maybe I don't need you anymore." To Moshi, Drakkon said, "Burn him to ash."

Before Moshi reached for him, Kraal said, "Will Tor go willingly? There's a reason you asked me. Tor knows me and knows my connection to Marcy. He will never listen to a Guardian."

Drakkon held up his hand, stopping Moshi. He studied Kraal then said to Moshi, "Take him to where he needs to go and don't let him out of your sight."

Kraal pushed himself up, the dizziness and sharp pains in his abdomen increasing. Moshi extended the blue mist and grunted for

Kraal to go first. Kraal refused to even glance at Drakkon, knowing that he'd be unable to hide the hatred he felt toward the Master of Darkness. *Freedom,* Kraal thought. *I want freedom. Please. I'll do whatever you want. Just get me out of this hellhole.* He wondered who he was talking to, but he knew. What he didn't know was whether he'd get the answer he desperately desired.

Michael's words echoed in his mind. *You have a lot more power than you realize.* But now, Kraal felt anything but powerful. He stepped through the blue mist and into the cold air of the Himalayans.

9

DEBORAH

Deborah picked up the Mathilde impostor and threw it over her shoulder. "We have to get you out of here." She moved through the cave and saw Eli waiting for her at the entrance. He handed her a bag of supplies. "Michael had to leave."

"Yes," she said without saying anything more. She wasn't about to reveal any information to this creature pretending to be Mathilde. She nodded at Eli, said good-bye, then flew out of the protected sanctuary. She already planned on heading back to the abandoned house where she and Michael found Kraal and Mathilde. If there were clues to what happened to Mathilde, they would be there.

Deborah found the abandoned farmhouse easily enough and set down the Mathilde impostor next to the well. "Do you need to drink? I thought you might be thirsty." The impostor shook its head. "Interesting. Normally a Shadow develops an unquenchable thirst if they stay in the mortal realm too long."

Since leaving the sanctuary, Deborah wracked her memory for a creature in hell that could shapeshift. Other than Drakkon who only morphed into dragon or human, she couldn't recall anything else. But she hadn't even experienced half of hell. Who knew what other creatures existed. And it would be like Drakkon to do something like this.

"Stay here. I'm going to check the perimeter." She ascended straight into the air and scanned the scene. What she really needed to do was think. This way, she could keep an eye on the impostor while trying to work out a plan.

Deborah thought about how to best find Mathilde, but another thought wouldn't leave her alone. *What if she's dead?*

No. She wouldn't think about that scenario. She would do what she could to find her and free her.

Any plan she concocted, Deborah couldn't see how she'd avoid hell. All plans led to her storming the gates and demanding Mathilde. Angels were already on assignment. And she technically was a light-bearer like Eli and others. Angels were created as such. They had never been mortals. Light-bearers, however, had been mortals approved for divine tasks in the afterlife. She commanded authority, but not enough to alter the assignments of others. Her assignment had been simple: protect the human anomaly at all costs.

And she had failed.

The way she looked at it was that it was up to her to fix it. Michael wanted to help, and she loved him for it, but this wasn't his battle. He had already sacrificed over twenty mortal years to occupy hell to free her and Tor. As an archangel, he had a lot of work to do, and he was rather consumed with her.

Deborah needed to release him from this responsibility of protecting her.

"What a mess," she said to the sky. "And it's my mess. All of it."

She caught the impostor's movement and saw the façade slightly flicker. All of her frustration over her mistakes reached their breaking point. She descended, landing quickly right beside the impostor. "What are you doing? Do you need something?"

"I'm thirsty now," it said, sounding just like Mathilde.

"Well, let me get you some water. I'll pump, and you drink." Deborah moved to the pump, her eyes never leaving the impostor.

"So, what's your plan now?" it asked while slowly licking at the water as it poured out. "Seeing as I'm rejected from the holy forest or whatever it is."

Deborah stopped pumping and gave a half-smile. "I'm working it out. Actually, I'm surprised that you refused to get rid of the evil seed inside of you."

The impostor sat back and wiped its mouth.

Deborah tried another angle. "Remember when we'd get so thirsty that we'd sneak off and steal fountain drinks from local gas stations?" Deborah watched to see if the impostor had any reaction. "What was the name of that one weird gas station in Oklahoma?"

The impostor said nothing.

Irritation brewed inside Deborah. The real Mathilde would know the answer because it was one of their favorite memories. The frozen Coke machine broke, and they had tried to turn it off but to no avail. The cold slush poured and poured out of it. The grief was so intense that it nearly took Deborah's breath away. "It's one of our favorite memories," she said, becoming weary of playing games. What she desired was to find Mathilde.

She heard the snakes before she saw them. Glancing at the impostor, she noted the small smile on its face. Deborah sprang into action, throwing herself on the impostor and pinning it to the ground. She had to remind herself it wasn't Mathilde as she put her sword to its neck. "Where is she?" she yelled.

The impostor grinned, a lizard tongue flicking out of its mouth.

"Tell me or you die."

"Then you'll never know," it said while still flicking its tongue at her.

The snakes slithered out of the grass, racing toward her. Deborah grabbed the impostor and flew up into the air. Holding it by its neck, she said, "Where is she? I won't ask again."

The impostor shifted in such a way that Deborah could see the lizard-man for a moment. Then it shifted to look exactly like Deborah. "We're going to kill all humanity," the impostor said, sounding just like Deborah's voice. "And it's all your fault. Can you do anything right?"

Shame and anger mixed into rage, and Deborah shoved her sword into it. It turned back to being a lizard-man for a second before turning to ash. The rage had yet to let up, so she swooped down and landed amid the snakes. She killed every last one, ash surrounding her.

Still emotional, she shot up into the sky. Letting the emotions overtake her, she let the tears come. It was her fault. All of it. And now Mathilde was missing or dead. The tears turned to sobs.

DEBORAH FLEW from one town to another, scouting out the groups of Shadow trainees that should be out on their training sessions. It was the dead of night, and that's when the creatures of hell came out to play. But the towns had very little Shadow activity. A few Elder Shadows emerged from dark crevices here and there with their Guardian close by. She kept her distance, not wanting to alarm them or for Drakkon to get word that she was searching for Mathilde. But where were the trainees?

Eventually the night ushered out the same demonic bugs who attacked her not too long ago. Had that only been weeks earlier in the mortal realm? She observed as sets of them morphed into small imps and crawled through bedroom windows.

Needing answers, she decided that cornering them may be her best bet. She thought about calling out for Michael to help, but he needed to secure the sanctuaries. Besides, she could destroy the entire pack of these evil miscreants. And she needed answers.

She descended until her feet touched the city block. As soon as she did, every little imp turned its head in her direction. Last time when she was discovered, they moved toward her, but this time, they let out a collective screech and ran away from her. But they weren't fast enough.

Deborah flew and grabbed one who squealed. Others stopped and squealed in unison. She remembered that they were many parts of one hellish creature. "I need to talk to you. Now!" She twisted the imp's arm when suddenly all of them burst into thousands of black beetles. They scurried off until they came together forming the shape of a man. He spoke fast in a foreign tongue, all the voices merging into one.

"Where are the Shadow trainees?" she asked, closing the distance between them.

He kept speaking gibberish.

"I asked you a question." She unsheathed her sword. "I've already used this tonight. Don't make me use it again."

"Death," it hissed. "You have brought death upon them."

The words startled her. "D-Death?"

Suddenly, the man exploded, and the chaotic beetles completely covered Deborah.

You did it, they chanted in unison while they swarmed her. *You killed your kind.*

Deborah released the light from inside of her, zapping the bug creatures. Once again, she found herself covered in ash.

She fell to her knees, the weight of Shadow deaths weighing even more heavily on her. "What am I to do?" she prayed, needing direction. "I made a mess of everything. Blood is on my hands. Please help."

The light burned intensely inside, and she took a moment to appreciate the sense of calm it provided her.

Deborah sensed she was being watched. Sighing, she took out her sword ready for another attack. When she surveyed the area, there was nothing out of the ordinary. She stood and checked again. Out of the corner of her eye, she caught movement in the shadows. She didn't move, and instead used her senses to see where the Shadow was going. She turned to the right and saw an Elder Shadow at the edge of a shadow beside a thicket of trees. His back was hunched over, and his gray hair hung limply like loose strings. Deborah felt an overwhelming sense of compassion. *Are you all right?* She projected her question to him, hoping he had the ability to project thoughts.

I haven't been slaughtered like many others. The Shadows' time draws to a close. We will be exterminated soon. But right now, I'm still of some use.

Is it true then? Shadows are being killed?

The Elder Shadows still serve a purpose, but not the young ones. Most of the trainees are dead. A few are kept in cages. He's killing them off one-by-one.

Have you heard about a Shadow trainee that goes by Mathilde? Hell was huge, but maybe this Elder Shadow had heard of her. Deborah had to take that chance.

No, but if she's a trainee, then she's probably dead. If she's not dead, then she's in the cages and will be soon.

Deborah took a sharp breath. All her friends...dead? One of Drakkon's Guardians appeared beside the Elder Shadow. Deborah watched as the enormous Guardian grabbed the Elder Shadow berating him.

"No," she said, flying so fast, she was upon the Guardian before he knew what hit him. "Leave the Shadow alone!" Her sword at his neck, she said through gritted teeth, "You're done torturing Shadows."

"It doesn't matter," the Elder Shadow said. "I'm as good as dead as soon as Drakkon finds out you tried to protect me."

The Guardian grinned belligerently and then threw Deborah off him. Taken by surprise, she fell against a tree. The Guardian extended the blue mist while grabbing the Elder Shadow. The Shadow would be killed for helping her. Deborah was once again responsible for another life lost.

"No!" she yelled, flying straight at them. No more Shadows would die because of her.

The Guardian noticed her, but it was too late.

Deborah flew right into the blue mist and back into hell.

1 0

TOR

Tor sat up fast, muffling the scream into the blanket. Another nightmare. But it wasn't a nightmare. It was real. He was back in hell. Only this time, he wasn't controlling the fire. The fire was consuming him. Marcy was also there, reaching out to save him, but she was out of grasp. And then he fell into the inferno as the flames devoured him whole. He got up from the bed and drank heartily from the water pitcher. He never could seem to quench his thirst.

Knowing sleep would not come back, he threw on a shirt from the pile Lin delivered the day before. It was scratchy and ugly, and it would burn up quickly. Oh well, he wasn't too sure what he thought about fire, not after watching his father shrink back in terror. Had he really appeared that evil? Is that how he had looked his whole life? Tor had gone to Timothy just as Samson instructed and was even reasonably successful at apologizing, but it still bothered him. He desired the power he had from before, but for the first time, he saw the cost involved. And he didn't like it.

He slipped out of his makeshift room and decided to explore what he quickly figured out was a rather massive sanctuary hidden near the top of a mountain. Samson had given him a tour of most of it, but Tor needed to move and think. He'd been training these last few days with Samson and making fast progress. But the energy inside of him still seemed subdued since the fire incident.

He passed Timothy's room and heard his father's snores. He felt a tug within that he hadn't experienced until recently. Anytime he came to the mortal realm from hell, he despised the closeness of families. Now he understood the intense jealousy and that he hadn't despised them. He had longed for the developed bond within a family unit. It's why—when no one was looking—he couldn't help but save children from the clutches of his weather terrors. A bond was developing between him and his father, and he wanted to do whatever he could not to break that bond.

Tor found himself back in the alcove that housed the fresh spring. He sat at the water's edge and leaned back admiring the crystals reflecting the moon's light. As minutes turned into an hour, his breathing slowed and relaxed, and his heart settled into a contented rhythm. "So, this is what peace feels like," he murmured to himself. His eyelids drooping, Tor began to drift off again to sleep.

Tor. The voice seemed far away, so far away that Tor could barely hear it. *Tor.*

"Tor. Wake up."

Tor awoke to Samson shaking him vigorously. He had a biting comment, but he noticed Sam's furrowed brow and understood the urgency. He sat up quickly, wiping the heavy sleep from his eyes. "What's wrong? Did something happen?"

"We have a situation. Did you hear someone calling for you?"

"Yes. In my dream. The voice was far away."

"I heard it too. It wasn't a dream."

"Is someone outside the cave? No one can find this place, right? No one from hell?" Tor jumped up and began to pace.

"Whoever it is isn't in the sanctuary. That's what is alarming. They are communicating to you from outside of it."

Tor.

A chill shot down Tor's spine, and goosebumps erupted. Tor rubbed his arms, annoyed at another human trait showing up at an inconvenient time. "Is someone at the cave's entrance? But how could their voice reach me?"

"He's not calling your name out loud," Samson said quietly, still listening.

"A Shadow?" The energy inside hummed in response. "Some Shadows can communicate telepathically. Only the very skilled."

Samson frowned. "They've found you."

"How? I thought these sanctuaries are hidden."

Tor.

Samson ignored the voice and answered, "They are, but you were probably tracked. So, even if they don't have the exact location, they are close enough that this Shadow being is trying to contact you. He still seems to be trying to locate you, which means the Shadow can't hear us."

"I can communicate my thoughts telepathically. He could hear my thoughts if I let him."

"No. The last thing we need is for you to be manipulated and tricked into leaving the sanctuary."

"What makes you think I'd be easily manipulated? I know Drakkon's tactics better than anyone."

"Because he doesn't play fair. And if you know his tactics better than anyone, then you know what he's willing to do to get you. Think about Timothy. If he figures out who Timothy is and who he is to you, then he will use that to his advantage."

Tor nodded. "You're right. Timothy must be protected at all costs. What's the plan?"

"Let me investigate. You stay here, and no matter what, do not step out of the sanctuary."

"I did that once in Ireland and was beaten to a bloody pulp. Trust me, I have no desire to relive that."

Samson nodded then disappeared right in front of Tor. Eli could do the same thing. Tor used to be able to do something like that, but that was *before*. Tor pulled the loose tunic down and examined the scar over his heart. He touched it gently, outlining its marking. He vividly remembered Eli and his fight. He was no match for Eli, and the sword of truth sliced through him, killing the evil seed that had been planted within him. "I don't want to go back," he said the words aloud, feeling surer of it than he ever had before. "I only wish I knew what I was supposed to do."

Tor.

"No," he said, pressing his hands to his ears. "I will not respond." He glanced at the water and wondered if being submerged would make the voice stop. Without another thought, he jumped into the cold water. This time the water didn't shoot him out. Instead, it heavily pushed him down to the bottom. Tor tried to kick his way to the water's surface, but the water had a mind of its own, trapping him at the bottom. At first, he didn't panic, choosing to investigate the clear bottom of this spring, seeing if there was some channel or pathway to the surface. Being an inhabitant of both realms allowed him more time without oxygen. Eventually though, he felt the burning in his lungs and knew he needed air. But the water wasn't releasing him. It was like a wall surrounding him, and no matter how hard he tried, he couldn't kick or swim past it.

The energy inside swelled, and Tor would have felt relief if he hadn't been drowning. He used to control the elements, but they never had a mind of their own. Feeling the fatigue from oxygen depletion, Tor focused on the energy surge within him. *Release me!*

Immediately, the water shot him up and out, and Tor landed with a thud on the rocky ground.

He coughed and sputtered until he could reasonably breathe again. Tor turned to the water and yelled, "What was that?"

Strangely, the water rippled in a circular pattern.

"Did the water just answer you?"

Tor saw Timothy approach. "It tried to kill me."

The water rippled again briefly.

"I saw you come out of the water. It was as if the water placed you on the edge. Why would it try to kill you then push you out?"

"Good question." Tor still glared at the crystal-clear spring. The energy had yet to dissipate. "It dragged me all the way to the bottom, which is much deeper than you think, then it wouldn't let me swim back up. It was like a water wall."

Timothy knelt and placed his hand in the spring. "It's cold but clear. Very beautiful." He looked up at Tor. "If it kept you trapped at the bottom, how did you get out?"

"I don't know. The energy inside me was racing, as if it was trying to get out. It must have sensed that I was suffering from oxygen depletion. Then I told the water to release me, and it shot up and out like a cannon."

"The water obeyed you?"

"I don't know that it heard me. I thought of the words. I didn't actually say them. My reasoning is the energy from inside me pushed itself out, catapulting me onto the dry ground."

Timothy wiped his hands on his trousers and stood up. "Hmm. I have an idea. Try to compel the water like you did the fire. The fire responded to your anger. Maybe the water has responded to you too."

Tor was tempted. The ability to control the elements meant that his power would be mostly returned. But what if he couldn't control it fully? What if it scared his father again? "I want to try, but I don't want to be who I once was. I'm conflicted."

"Before being set free, you used your powers for evil, but Tor, you have been set free." Timothy touched Tor's arm. "It's time you practice using these gifts you've been given for good."

"I don't know how to do that. Controlling fire scared you. What if controlling water drowns you?"

"I trust you, son. I'm not necessarily afraid of you. But I don't like what you've experienced, and what it did to you." Timothy glanced around. "Maybe Samson can offer some insight."

"He's out investigating something." Tor paused, realizing for the first time since jumping into the water, he could no longer hear the voice calling for him.

"What is it? Is everything all right?"

"Did you hear someone calling out to me? It was very faint."

Timothy paled and shook his head. "Someone's calling your name? Who was it?"

"Samson went to check it out. He told me to stay here and not to leave the sanctuary under any circumstances." Now Tor shook his head. "You know, before all of this happened to me, I would have balked at someone giving me an order. I'd have stormed out of here and did my thing."

"What changed?"

"Nearly losing my life and being worried about what Drakkon would do to Marcy. That's the thing with Drakkon, he will hurt you by hurting those you care about. He enjoys it. I know I'm not ready to face him, so I'm actually going to listen to Samson's directive."

"Interesting. Any you think whoever is calling you is from… hell?"

"Yes, I know it. I feel it. Some Elder Shadows can communicate into your thoughts. That's what it was. I'm positive."

"Then you've run out of time. No more wondering about your giftings. You need to train."

"I *am* training. With Samson. You've seen us. I'm a skilled fighter, and fighting Samson is no joke. But I'm holding my own. That says something."

"That's not what I'm talking about. I'm talking about opening yourself up to all that is yours." Timothy stepped closer to Tor. He looked from the water to Tor. "Don't worry. I'm not going to let anything happen to you. But I have a hunch that you need a little help."

"What are you talking about—" but Tor couldn't finish. Timothy shoved him as hard as he could into the water. Tor tried to stand up since he was still in the shallow end, but the water swirled around him, grabbing his arms and dragging him down to the deep bottom. Tor saw Timothy through the water peering into it.

"You can control it," Timothy said.

The energy inside of him hummed loudly, and Tor focused on what it was doing. There was a rhythm to the energy, vibrations that seemed to be communicating something. This time, Tor refused to panic. Timothy was right. The energy and the water were communicating with him. He wasn't sure what was being said, but there seemed to be an expectation as if both the energy and water were expecting something from him. *Let me go*, he directed his thoughts to the water. Immediately, the water released him. This time, it didn't catapult him out of it. The water seemed to wait for the next directive.

Tor lay himself flat at the bottom of the spring. *Bring me to the surface*, he thought the words and smiled as the water pushed him up to the surface. "Take me to my father." The water lifted him to a standing position, then moved toward the water's edge, setting him squarely on the ground before pulling itself back into the spring.

Timothy's eyes were round and shining. "Unbelievable."

Tor hadn't stopped smiling. "It didn't just obey me. It knew what I wanted it to do. This time I didn't want it to throw me out. I wanted it to gently release me to the surface. But I never thought those words. Just visualized what I wanted, and it happened. The same thing with bringing me to you. It did exactly what I envisioned." Tor paused, and a frown replaced his grin.

"What? Isn't this a good thing? Why the frown?"

"It's like before. Under Drakkon, I didn't think about any of my powers, I simply had them, and the elements obeyed."

"But it's not like before because *you're* different." Timothy pursed his lips. "I have another idea." He walked over to Samson's stove contraption. "I'm going to set my clothing on fire. You use the water to put out the fire."

"No!" Tor yelled it so loudly that Timothy stopped. "You are not going to play with fire. That may not work as intended."

Timothy took off his shirt. "I wasn't talking about setting it on fire while wearing it. I'm going to set this shirt on fire, and let's see you drench it."

Tor turned to water and extended his hand. *Come to me.* Then Tor came up with an idea. He grinned as the water rose to a towering wave.

"Are you telling it to do that?" Timothy stared at the water, his burning shirt forgotten.

Tor's grin returned. "Drench him."

The water poured over Timothy and the stove contraption, extinguishing any fire and drenching Tor's father. "Tor!" Timothy said in exasperation.

Tor began to laugh. It felt strange and sounded foreign, which made him laugh even more.

Timothy marched over to the water and yelled at it, "Why'd you drench me? You need to drench him!" Suddenly, the water came up and blasted Tor, taking him off guard. He fell back and sat up sputtering. Timothy ran over to him in shock. "Son, I'm sorry. I didn't think the water would listen to me." He paused. "*Why* did it listen to me?"

"Do you feel something inside of you that burns but in a good way?" Tor let Timothy help him up.

"Yes, ever since you and I clasped hands, there has been some sort of energy inside of me. It's been lying low for the most part. I felt it when receiving the onslaught of your memories, I felt it strongly when you were covered in flames, and I felt it strongly when I shoved you in the water. Like it was compelling me to do it."

"Well, you are my father. I wonder if I get some of my abilities from you."

"Or if you somehow shared your abilities with me when we joined the covenant."

Both Tor and Timothy turned to the sound of rushing footsteps. The young woman, Lin, ran into the alcove, stopping at the sight of them. "Samson needs help."

Tor immediately raised his eyebrows. "Help with what?"

"Hell's minions arrived at one of the villages and are creating chaos. He can't be two places at once."

Tor didn't need the energy inside to vibrate in response to the lie. He could practically smell manipulation. "I'm not leaving the sanctuary."

"But Samson—" she whimpered, and for a moment, Tor hesitated. He felt her fear.

"We all know that Samson can defeat any demon in hell. Besides, he's a Guardian of this holy sanctuary. I don't think he can be killed a second time."

Lin wrung her hands and glanced behind her.

"Why don't you tell us what's really going on?" Timothy asked gently. He approached her. "Only honesty can be in this place, and your words are sounding like an ill-tuned note on an instrument."

Big tears formed in her eyes. "I'm not trying to manipulate or lie, but our village really does need help, and I can't find Samson anywhere."

"You said that Samson can't be two places at once. So, you already know that he's somewhere else."

11

KRAAL

Moshi hovered over Kraal. "It's cold here. Do what you need to do."

Kraal shivered, rubbing his hands across his arms. The weather didn't affect spirit beings like it did with humanity, but certain aspects of it were still unpleasant, especially the cold. Since spending so much time in the mortal realm, he was more susceptible to the elements than normal. Without some warmth, he'd freeze before the poison had its way. "Let me get us some warm clothes. If you wanted to start a fire, it'd help us warm up."

Before Kraal stepped into a shadow, Moshi stopped him. "Your comfort is not my priority."

"I can't think when I'm shivering. If I'm to do what we came to do, then I need to get warm."

Moshi sighed. "Such a pathetic Shadow. Your humanity is disgusting. I'm coming with you. And don't try anything stupid."

Kraal moved quickly in the shadows, relieved that there was a little more warmth within them. But not much. He stepped out of a shadow and into a village square complete with vendors lining the unpaved road. Live animals roamed among the clusters of mortals, but Kraal found what he was looking for. Several stalls sold knit scarves and hats, mittens and shawls. Taking a trick from Marcy, he slipped items on then stepped into a shadow before anyone could see. He grabbed a set of mittens, but before he could disappear, a woman grabbed his arm. "Demon," she whispered in a strange dialect. "You vanish before my eyes, but even demons must pay!"

She had captured the attention of others. Kraal looked straight into her eyes, as she became transfixed into the abyss. She screamed and let go of his arm. Kraal immediately hid in a shadow as others checked on the woman, but she was already too far gone. Kraal felt ashamed that he did that. He knew that humans couldn't stare into a Shadow's eyes or else face their greatest fears, losing themselves in the abyss behind his black orbs for eyes. But she had surprised him. Kraal noted that Marcy never got caught stealing.

As he moved quickly through the shadows out of the village, he thought of Marcy. He missed her. She had brought life to hell, and if he craved freedom before her, she only reinforced how desperately he needed freedom.

"Stop," Moshi ordered.

Kraal had felt his presence in the village and with him as he travelled, but with his thoughts on Marcy, he had momentarily forgotten about the gigantic Guardian. Kraal materialized next to a jutted rock's edge that would offer some protection from the harsh wind. He knelt beside the rock wall and tried to warm himself. The human materials helped, but there was a frigidness in the air that made it hard to breathe, let alone think. "Please...a fire would help me think. I'm not used to the cold."

"Did you say *please*?" Moshi scoffed. "Are you a proper Shadow now? This pathetic mortal realm is messing with your head. I actually enjoy watching you be miserable."

"I know you're cold too. It may not affect you like it does me, but you are uncomfortable. Don't deny it."

"I deny nothing. But I embrace the discomfort. I'm not weak like you." Moshi tilted his head and gave a sadistic smile. "It really is enjoyable watching you die. You know your lips are blue?"

"And if you go back without Tor? How will Drakkon handle it? You need me alive for the time being. So, a fire would be great."

Moshi growled in annoyance, flicked his wrist, and shot a fireball in front of Kraal. It's blaze increased. "I'm not going to keep it going for long. It'll need kindling. Go, get some."

Kraal could barely stand up. The cold plus the poison were a two-packed punch, and he still hadn't recovered from Drakkon's beating. But kindling would keep the fire without any more reliance on Moshi.

He remembered some chopped wood on the outskirts of the path leading to the village, so using evening shadows, he snuck as much wood as he could carry back to where Moshi's fire still blazed. The logs fell from his arms, crashing into the flames, as Kraal landed on his knees. His breathing was labored, but he couldn't think straight anymore. Even with the warmth of the fire, the pain from the poison only seemed to strengthen. Kraal rested his forehead on the ground.

"You have a job to do." Moshi used his pointed boot to push Kraal onto his back. "Get up and do what you came to do."

But Kraal couldn't move. "I'll work from down here," he

managed to say. "I'm going to try to communicate with Tor tele-pathically. If he's close by, I'll be able to reach him."

Moshi grunted and walked away. "I'm bored, so get it done."

Kraal opened his eyes and stared at the evening sky. The moon already found it's place there. He longed for so many things, but he wondered if death would find him first. But Michael had told him that the Nameless One wanted to help him. How could he? If he truly existed, and Kraal was unsure about that, how could he deliver Kraal from the most evil being to have ever existed?

You are not a slave. The words whispered in his head.

He tried to sit up to look around. Someone was communicating with him telepathically. *Tor?* He projected his thoughts, thinking of Tor. If Tor was within range, he may be able to hear Kraal's voice in his head. That was if the sanctuary didn't block it out. Kraal tried again. *Tor.*

You are not a slave. The words whispered again.

Tor? Can you hear me? Tor. Kraal paused. Whoever was speaking to him knew about his conversation with Michael and Eli. But without knowing who it was, he didn't know where to project his thoughts. *Who is this? Who is speaking to me?*

You are not a slave. Whoever it was only repeated the same statement.

Irritation brewed, and Kraal held up his shackled wrist. *Can you see this? This would suggest otherwise!* He focused his thoughts again on Tor, but his gaze stayed on the poisonous shackle. He took a shaky breath. If he was going to try to repeat what happened with Michael and Eli, he would need to do it quickly before Moshi caught on. He lay back down on the ground, stared at the darkening sky, and thought the words, *I am not a slave.* He paused, not feeling any different. *I am not a slave...I am not a slave...I am not a slave.* His breathing evened, his eyes closed. *I am not a slave.*

"What are you doing here?" Moshi asked some distance away.

"I was going to ask you the same question," a deep voice responded.

Kraal turned to see who had discovered them. Whoever it was could see Moshi, which meant it was from the spirit realm.

"Don't take another step closer," Moshi jeered. "Or you'll lose more than your eyes, Samson."

"Oh, you know me already? I didn't know we'd ever been introduced."

"Everyone knows about you. We laugh every time Delilah tells the story about how you pathetically believed all of her lies."

"Delilah's made a place for herself in hell? Of course, she has. I wouldn't expect anything less from a conniving, soulless woman. But that doesn't answer the question of what you're doing here."

"It's none of your business. We haven't touched your sanctuary."

"You're trying to communicate with someone inside the sanctuary, which makes it my business. Now leave while I'm asking nicely."

Moshi laughed humorlessly then drew his sword. "Last I checked I don't take orders from a blind light-bearer."

Kraal heard the guttural call from Moshi's low whistle and felt the ground beneath him start to tremble. He sighed impatiently. All hell was about to break loose. From the last attack he escaped, Kraal knew that light-bearers had more power than any demon in hell, but the demons would never admit it. Kraal felt the evil before seeing the first set of snakes slither past him. The ground opened up, swallowing the fire and nearly taking Kraal with it. He found a thick root protruding from the rock wall and hung on to it while an onslaught of imps climbed over each other to attack the light bearer first.

With the fire gone, Kraal could see the light-bearer standing amid hordes from hell. He noticed that the light-bearer was huge, much bigger than Eli and even had an edge over Michael. And he noticed that the light-bearer had no eyes, just sunken holes where eyes had been. Then he remembered the name Samson. Drakkon hated that name almost as much as the name of the Nameless One. Moshi had left out that Delilah was cast into the blazing inferno for all eternity, and he neglected to say that Samson got the last laugh in his own story.

Suddenly, Kraal felt compelled to help him. If he had to choose sides, he wanted to be on this guy's side. He might be blind, but he didn't seem worried or alarmed. Instead, he grinned at the demons as if he was going to enjoy the battle. But whereas this gigantic light-bearer and the demons were spirit-beings, Kraal being part human, would not fare as well. Still, he secretly rooted for Samson to win.

It was over almost as quickly as it began. Moshi stayed on the outskirts, watching Samson single-handedly defeating the mass of demons and imps attacking him. Kraal saw Moshi handle his sword, staying outside Samson's line of vision. The demons must have caught on to Moshi's strategy because they kept Samson' attention throwing themselves onto him and lashing out in intervals. Moshi disappeared only to reappear with his sword extended just behind Samson. Without thinking, Kraal projected a thought, hoping that the light-bearer could hear. *Behind you!*

Samson swiveled and blocked the sword, hitting Moshi so hard, his grip on the sword lessened just enough for Samson to grab it, flip it, and push it into Moshi's chest before Moshi knew what had happened. Kraal nearly laughed out loud at the evil Guardian's shocked expression right before he turned to ash.

Any relief Kraal felt was short-lived. Drakkon would be furious and would take it out on him. So lost in his thoughts, Kraal didn't see Samson approach until he stood directly beside him next to the jutted rock.

"That pit is huge," Samson said. "I'll need you out of the way, so I can close it up." Samson reached down, threw Kraal over his shoulder, and teleported to the other side of it. "Stay here."

Kraal tried not to stare too long at the blind man, although he didn't act like he was blind. Before he could respond, Samson teleported back to the rock wall and slammed his entire body into it. He heard a crack and thought it must be one of Samson's bones until Kraal saw the fracture in the rock expanding in multiple directions.

Samson hit the rock again with all his might before teleporting back to Kraal. "That should do it. How are you feeling?"

But Kraal's attention stayed on the now crumbling rock. There was a tremor when suddenly the entire rock wall crashed into the pit created by the imps. Turning to give this light-bearer his full attention, Kraal trembled at the power emanating from him. It reminded him of how Marcy looked when she remembered she was Deborah. The glow of her internal light showed in such a way that many of the demons in that battle actually ran away than to face her. Eli had the same light, but there was something about this blind man that Kraal found much more intimidating. "Wh-Who are you?"

"You already know. I'm Samson."

"Moshi knew you."

"Yes, I have a history with several legions in hell from when I was among the living in the mortal realm and a few times here and there within the past couple millennia. So, how are you holding up? We need to move quickly before Drakkon shows up with more. I'm not worried about myself, but you, on the other hand, he'll kill quickly."

"There's nowhere I can go where Drakkon won't find me."

"You can come with me, if you consent to killing the evil seed inside of you."

"As I explained to Eli and Michael, there's a small problem." Kraal held up his arm to display the poisonous shackle. Only it was gone.

"Are you referring to the shackle that is now buried underneath all that rumble? Because I'm not going after it."

At first, Kraal panicked. He jumped up and searched around him as if he'd find it and place it back on his wrist. Then he stopped and simply stared at his empty wrist. "It worked?"

"Yes. Now, do you agree to come with me, or would you rather stay here and meet your fate with the prince of darkness? Make sure you understand the implications. Coming with me means switching sides, and light cannot mix with darkness. That means we'd have a lot of work to do, and I'm not certain your body will tolerate the pain that is to come."

"Free from hell? I gladly accept." Kraal didn't need to think twice.

Both Samson and Kraal sensed the approaching darkness.

Samson grabbed Kraal and teleported right as a poisonous arrow flew past.

"He's mine!" Drakkon screamed, but they had already reappeared within the opening of the cave.

Samson set Kraal down. "You must walk in yourself without using any hellish tactic. So, no moving through shadows. Hurry."

Kraal didn't miss a beat; he ran into the cave feeling the darkness crawling toward him. He heard Samson outside the cave engaged in another attack. "I am not a slave," Kraal said out loud as he continued to run. He didn't know how long he should run before he was safe, but he didn't stop. Even when the natural light was gone, Kraal kept running.

An eerie scream echoed through the cave, growing louder and louder. "You're mine!"

"No! I am not a slave!" Kraal yelled. He rounded a corner and toppled into someone. Both lost their balance and fell onto the ground. Kraal hit and kicked with all he had in him. He was too close to freedom to lose now.

"Stop it!" the familiar voice ordered, throwing Kraal off him.

Kraal stumbled back. He was looking right at Tor.

12

TOR

"You." Tor didn't move. He stared at Kraal in shock and some contempt. So many memories flooded through his mind.

Timothy finally made it to them, stopping to catch his breath. "You're so fast," he panted.

Tor turned his attention to his father. "Sorry. When I heard the commotion, I didn't stop to wait for you."

Timothy glanced over at Kraal, then quickly shrank back. "Tor? I thought evil wasn't allowed in here."

"It's not." Tor said the words through gritted teeth. To Kraal, he asked, "What are you doing here? Darkness cannot mix with light."

"Samson saved me out there. I choose the light. I don't want to be a slave anymore. I'm not a slave. I'm free." Kraal touched his wrist where the shackle had been.

Tor ignored Kraal and put his arm around Timothy's shoulders, protecting him. Whispering, he said, "Go, and I'll stay here. And whatever you do, don't look into his eyes."

Timothy nodded and left them. Tor watched until his father was out of sight, then turned and faced Kraal. "You shouldn't be here."

"I'm not going to cause any trouble. I promise. I want the same thing you want."

"You promise? Please. You're an agent from hell. You can't fool me. And you don't know what I want."

"You want to be free. And you are. I want the same thing."

Tor shook his head. "No. Not here. I need to talk to Samson."

Samson materialized beside him. "You need to talk to me? About what?" He glanced over at Kraal and said, "I've never seen that before in my entire existence. There is something special about you."

"What did you see?" Tor asked. "And what is special about Kraal? Other than he kidnaps newborns from their families, sending the baby into the depths of hell."

"Easy," Samson warned Tor. "Don't get angry. It brings out the fire in you, and we're still learning how to contain it. Deep breaths."

Tor's eye twitched. "Stop telling me to calm down. I'm not angry, but I do want to know what's so special about this demon?"

Samson grabbed Kraal's wrist and held it up for Tor to examine. "This. Do you see a poisonous shackle on his wrist?"

Tor looked from Kraal's wrist to Samson. "No. Is one supposed to be there?"

"There was one there, but Kraal broke free from it. All by himself."

Tor's eyes widened in surprise. "How'd you do *that?*" he asked Kraal in an accusing tone.

Kraal stared at his wrist and shrugged. "I don't know. Michael and Eli told me that my humanity made me more powerful than I imagined. I didn't believe them, but this...*happened.*"

"I am so confused," Tor said, feeling the irritation grow. "Humanity doesn't make you powerful. It makes you weak."

"No." Kraal met Tor's gaze. "We've been told that, but it's a lie. Humanity has free will. I'm descended from humans. You're human. That's why Drakkon can't control us. We realized that we can be free from him."

"Do you realize what that means for the others?" Samson asked excitedly. He rubbed his hands together in anticipation. "If there are other Shadows as you all call them, then they can be free. They don't have to be enslaved to Drakkon anymore. And you, Kraal, showed us how simply it can be done."

Tor mulled over the information. "That doesn't explain how you are here, or what happened to the poisonous shackle."

"I told myself that I'm not a slave. That's it. I had to focus a bit and really think about the words, but I didn't even realize the shackle had fallen off until Samson pointed it out."

"Which is why he's here," Samson said to Tor. "Now if you excuse us, Kraal and I have a date with death."

Tor shook his head. *This can't happen,* he thought.

It is meant to be. Kraal is supposed to be here. Samson led Kraal down one of the tunnels leading away from Tor and Timothy's rooms.

"He kidnapped me!" Tor yelled, no longer communicating telepathically. He felt the fire rise in him, and he released it, desiring to throw a massive fireball at Kraal. "He ruined my life! I was tortured and abused and ripped from my family! I never met my mother because of *him!*"

Samson turned around, caught the fireball, extinguished it, and pointed at Tor. "Your clothes are burned up. You'll need to deal with that. We'll deal with the rest later."

Tor looked down at his nakedness and sighed. He hated human clothes.

AFTER FINDING another hideous human outfit, Tor found Timothy kneeling beside his bed. His eyes were closed, and he whispered fervently. Tor could pick out some of the phrases. "Save him from destruction...deliver him from evil...remind him he is loved..."

Tor had experienced enough in the mortal realm to know what prayer looks like. It didn't surprise him to see Timothy pray, but it did make him feel uncomfortable. Tor had a suspicion that Timothy was praying for him. He cleared his throat, and Timothy paused and turned around.

"I'm nearly finished," Timothy said. He patted the ground beside himself. "Come and kneel with me."

Tor considered the request before walking into the room and kneeling beside his father.

"New outfit?" Timothy asked. "This one looks like someone sowed grass together."

"I sort of torched the other outfit. I think they're running out of clothes."

Timothy chuckled. "Oh goodness, what happened?"

"I got angry. That definitely brings out the fire." Tor sighed, then admitted, "I don't know what to do with all this anger I feel. Like that Shadow who is here now. That's Kraal. The

Shadow who took me from you when I was a baby. Because of him, I never met my mother. Because of him, I was stuck in hell." Tor felt the heat build inside of himself. He took deep breaths to calm his emotions. "I'm angry, and I want to retaliate. But I know I can't. This makes everything so complicated. Like I want to do good. I want to *be* good, but I don't know what to do with the anger."

Timothy took Tor's hand in his. "That evil being is your kidnapper?"

"Yes."

The two of them sat quietly for some time. "Oh my," Timothy finally said. "This is a test, but I'm not sure I will pass it."

Tor heard the catch in Timothy's voice and observed his father's struggle to keep his emotions in check. But Timothy couldn't stop the tear that traveled down his face. The realization hit Tor like an arrow to his forehead. "I shouldn't have told you. I didn't think how the news would affect you."

Timothy wiped his eyes and sniffed. "There was something about him I didn't like. Now I know. He took my son from me."

"Yes," Tor said barely above a whisper. "What are we going to do?"

"I don't know." Timothy studied Tor with such sorrow on his features that it looked like he might weep at any moment. "Will you stay here with me and pray? I don't want to be alone right now. I...I don't trust myself."

Tor nodded. "I'm not entirely sure how to pray, but I've seen mortals do it. I can figure it out." Tor left out that he wasn't sold on praying to some eternal deity who allowed him to be kidnapped and tortured for twenty years.

"Sometimes you don't have to say anything. Sometimes it's just talking to God in your heart."

Tor nodded again. He watched as Timothy closed his eyes and bowed his head. This time, no words came out, but Timothy's tears were released. Tor felt helpless as his father cried. So, Tor stayed. In a gesture, foreign to him, he placed his arm around his father's shoulders.

13

DEBORAH

"Get your filthy hands off him." Deborah had once again pinned the Guardian to the ground. This time she was ready and used her power to truly hold him in place. He couldn't move.

He began to laugh, and then others around them laughed and jeered. Deborah didn't have to glance up to know where she'd landed. The evil was palpable in Drakkon's throne room, more so now that she remembered who she was. And the light within her blazed. She couldn't hide herself if she wanted. Luckily, she didn't care.

She stood up, keeping the Guardian paralyzed. And she stared right into the eyes of the prince of darkness. "Look who it is," she said. "The overlord himself. Although, I'm no longer afraid of your presence. Actually, I wouldn't mind defeating you again."

Drakkon moved toward her slowly. He showed no fear. If anything, he acted satisfied as if he finally got what he wanted. "If it isn't *Marcy*. The Shadow girl with the blue eyes. Welcome back."

"This place was never my home. I came with a purpose, and I finished what I started. Tor is gone. Now, I'm here to free the Shadows, starting with Mathilde. Where is she? And think twice before playing dumb."

Drakkon glanced down at Deborah's extended sword pointing directly at his neck. "Oh, I am many things, but dumb isn't one of them."

"It's dumb to think you even have a chance at the white throne. You know it. You are stuck in this hellhole until the end of time."

"That is no way to speak to the one who holds your friend's life on a thread." Drakkon pressed into the sword, glaring at Deborah.

"She's alive?" Deborah dropped the sword. "Tell me where she is, and I'll refrain from leveling hell to nothing but ash."

Drakkon chuckled, then looked around to the vile creatures who littered his throne room. "Can you believe the nerve of this lightbearer? She comes to my kingdom, and then she proceeds to threaten to kill us. But will we allow her to tell us what to do?"

The creatures responded in frenzied paranoia with screeches and guttural sounds, making Deborah's spine chill. One of the creatures was another lizard-man, much like the one Deborah had killed. He stared right at her, then morphed into a replica of herself. "You don't have a choice."

"Oh yes, I do. You see, *you* are not supposed to be here. That's why there is such chaos already. You and the horrible archangel disguised yourselves and inhabited my kingdom. That breaks the rules. And yet, here you are again. Breaking the rules established by your master. There are consequences for breaking the rules."

"Stop trying to manipulate me. You can't touch me, and you

know it. I, on the other hand, can destroy every creature in hell. And don't think I won't. So, give me Mathilde, and we'll be on our way."

Drakkon laughed. "This is so beautiful. Storming into my kingdom, telling me what to do. You're no Michael. And you have limitations, which you'll find out soon enough."

Deborah scoffed. "I'm done talking. Where is Mathilde?"

"Tell you what. I will allow you access to all the levels of hell, even the ones you've never experienced. If you find Mathilde, you get to keep her. But you cannot touch any of my creatures while here. Deal?"

"I don't make deals with the devil." Deborah took another look around the room. Each creature kept their distance, which reassured her somewhat. But she wasn't kidding herself. Trying to find Mathilde in hell was a massive undertaking. Drakkon's kingdom housed all the unrepentant souls of deceased mortals plus an innumerable number of demons and imps. But she didn't want to create more chaos than necessary, especially since she had made another rash decision outside of any clear directive. "I will leave your soldiers and underlings alone, so long as they don't interfere with my task or bother me in anyway."

Drakkon nodded in agreement. "See? That wasn't so bad. Could you release Malak now? You still have him paralyzed."

The energy buzzed loudly, and Deborah understood the warning. But she also had to find Mathilde. *Please,* she prayed silently. *Forgive me for my rash actions and help me find my friend.* She didn't receive the sense of calm that comes when praying. Then again, she was in hell, doing exactly what she told Michael she wasn't going to do. Sighing, she released the Guardian.

"Now, go about your business. I have some work to do that you will probably find unpleasant."

Deborah saw Drakkon signal the Guardian, Malak. He jumped up, and without missing a beat, he pulled out his sword and grabbed the Elder Shadow.

"No more Shadows die!" Deborah declared, pulling the Shadow to her, and stepping in front of him.

Drakkon gave a humorless laugh. "You pathetic creature. You don't tell me what to do in my kingdom!"

The Elder Shadow gasped behind her. Deborah turned quickly, her sword unsheathed, but she was too late. The Guardian had burned him to ash.

"It's sad, really," Drakkon said to Deborah. "This one had some incredible abilities, much like your mentor, Kraal. But any of my creatures tainted by you will die. And that includes every little pesky trainee."

Fury shook her, but Drakkon would only revel in any reaction from her. "You'll regret that," she said through gritted teeth.

"I don't think I will." Drakkon approached her. "I'm going to kill everyone close to you, and if I'm lucky, you'll be there to watch. You don't have the upper hand this time. My kingdom, my rules. And your precious archangel doesn't even know you're here. I've kept him busy with my assault on your precious angelic sanctuaries."

Deborah thought of the creature that infiltrated Eli's forest. "There are others?" The realization that Michael wouldn't be available to save her this time hit her hard. She should be with him, helping him protect the holy sanctuaries, and instead, she headed straight back into hell. Drakkon's laughter at her situation brought her back to the present. She frowned and suddenly flew past

Drakkon to the waterfall, needing to get away from the prince of darkness so that she could think.

The rising panic was there, but that was Marcy, not Deborah. "Get a rip," she told herself. "You are not helpless." The energy within in hummed in approval as if fueling her reserves. She moved quickly, choosing to head to the bottom-most level of hell: the lake of fire. She needed to free the trainees from those torturous cages and find out if they knew anything about Mathilde. But would that lead to their death? Either way they had a death sentence. At least this way, she could try to protect them, and maybe they could help her find Mathilde.

Before she would have had no idea where anything was, but now, the light inside easily directed her. That, and the screams coming from the pit could also be heard.

Deborah stepped down on the fire pit's ledge and immediately stepped back. The agony of its occupants nearly made her weep. The darkness pressed in but the light within her kept it at bay. She was thankful that the light still stayed with her, guiding her, and protecting her.

"Marcy!" someone called out.

Deborah easily spotted the cages that now dangled over the inferno. "Arec?"

The Shadow trainee along with several others occupied one of the cages. Deborah counted the number of cages. Nine cages filled with Shadow trainees. And now they all called out to her. "Marcy! Save us!"

A growl came from behind her, and she turned to see a gargantuan wolf-man licking its lips. It looked like the one Michael had killed when he was disguised as Lynde. "If you come near me, you die. If you come near them, you die." She shoved past him to the ropes and yanked with all she had. Her strength might not have been the same as Michael's, but it surged through her all the same, and in no time, she had brought the cage back to the ledge. As soon as she sliced through the lock to its door, she began yanking on the rope for the next cage. Eventually, all cages and the occupants were secure on the ledge.

"Look at you," Arec said in awe. The others surrounded Deborah, all seemingly mesmerized at the light that emanated from her. "You really are an angel of light."

"Technically, I'm a light-bearer. I was once human but earned eternal light. But we're called angels of light a lot." Deborah stopped talking. The last thing they needed was a definition.

"What were you when you were with us?"

"Mostly human, I think. I was rebirthed in a human shell so that I could save Tor. He was stolen as an infant, and I came to hell to retrieve him."

All of them still acted amazed. Suddenly, Arec threw his arms around her. "You'll always be Marcy to me. Thanks for saving us." Others followed and hugged her.

Deborah watched as the wolf-man and others of his kind slowly moved toward them. "We must hurry. Do any of you know where Mathilde is? Drakkon took her and hid her, but I have no idea where."

None of them seemed to know. Arec answered, "I haven't seen her since you left. Drakkon came and snatched her almost immediately afterward."

"All right." Deborah hid her disappointment. This task seemed near impossible, but at the moment, she needed to get these

Shadow trainees somewhere safer than this fire pit. "We need to go somewhere safe."

"It's hell," a trainee said. "Nowhere is safe."

"What about Levea? At least we won't be surrounded by these wolf creatures who are drooling right now, waiting to attack." Deborah waited for any of the trainees to respond.

"Sounds good to us." Arec glanced around, then asked hesitantly, "How are we going to get there? We can't move between levels without a Guardian. Can you do it instead?"

Deborah's heart seized for a moment as the realization hit her. She never had the power to leave hell for the mortal realm. Guardians could extend their arm and create the blue mist, but Deborah never had a need to do it. And light-bearers didn't have access to hell. It wasn't a place for them to ever visit. Until her. Until now. She extended her hand now and willed the blue mist to appear.

"Can you not access the other levels at least?" Arec asked quietly.

"Yes, by flying. I can maybe carry one or two of you at a time, but there are at least three dozen of you. I'd have to make trips." Deborah tried to act calm, but she understood why the wolf creatures were surrounding them. They knew she couldn't take them all. As soon as she left to transfer a couple trainees to Levea, the rest would be slaughtered. Drakkon's words replayed in her mind. *Any of my creatures tainted by you will die. And that includes every little pesky trainee.* "This is what he meant."

"Are you leaving soon?" the wolf-man taunted. "We are hungry for a snack."

A few of the younger trainees whimpered.

Deborah unsheathed her sword. To the wolf-man, she said, "Or I kill all of you now."

"You don't scare us. If we die, more of us come out to finish the job." The disdain in his voice irritated her. They truly weren't afraid. Deborah was on their turf, and even with her supernatural power and ability, she was seriously outnumbered already.

A thought came to her, and she nearly sighed in relief. To the Shadow trainees, she said, "I've got an idea. I think I can manage flying two of you out of here. The rest of you need to split up and step into their shadows." The trainees murmured in confusion. They've never shared shadow space with others. "Trust me, it can be done. Your clothes have shadows. Step into it, and then make room for others. The space will be tight, but we have to make it work."

Deborah picked Arec and Dimitri, another male trainee, who were larger than the others. This would provide more available shadow space through their clothing. When the wolf creatures saw that the plan was actually working, they became agitated, shoving at each other and howling in intervals. One snatched a trainee right as she was stepping into Arec's shadow. Deborah sliced off his arm. "Leave them alone."

Suddenly, the wolf creatures lunged at her, knocking her sword out of her hand. One bit into her shoulder before she evoked her protection shield. She pushed past the pain, knowing her body would heal itself. She held out her hand, and the sword flew back into it. Energy shot through her, knocking them down like bowling pins.

Deborah quickly grabbed the hands of the two Shadow trainees. "Is everyone on board?"

They nodded, watching her with awe.

"Then let's not waste any more time." She levitated with them, trying to get used to their weight. She felt the strain of two full-size young men hanging onto her, but it was manageable. She flew to the waterfall then shot up, moving as quickly as she could.

They reached Levea, which resembled a deserted wasteland.

"Where'd they all go?" she asked, already knowing the answer.

She set the two trainees down and turned quickly to hide her horror-filled expression. All the trainees were *gone.* Deborah covered her mouth to stifle the grief.

Arec approached her. "Can the other trainees step out of our shadows now?"

Deborah nodded, then asked, "No one was left here?"

"He threw your group in the cages over the fiery pit, but first he had us watch. He killed them all. Even sent Rakye through to take many of their souls." Arec's bottom lip trembled. As the other trainees materialized from the shadows of his clothing, they too took one look at their abandoned home and became visibly emotional.

Deborah knew that Shadows couldn't cry. But she didn't need to see the tears to feel their grief. Knowing that they were not safe, she shook herself from the sorrow. She'd have to grieve this horrendous loss later. "We need to figure out how to get out of here."

"You don't have access to both realms?"

"Yes and no. I can access the new city where light-bearers live and congregate when not on duty, and I can access the mortal realm and all the spiritual sanctuaries within it."

"But what about hell? How did you get here?" Arec seemed genuinely curious.

"I've never accessed hell. I never needed to. That wasn't the job of light-bearers. The first time I accessed it was through Kraal, and he probably had some Guardian let us through. I don't remember because I had been reborn as a human infant."

"And this time? How'd you get here to rescue us in this moment?"

Deborah's heart sank. "I followed a Guardian and Elder Shadow. The Guardian had extended the blue mist for them to walk through, and I took that opportunity to fly into the mist. My only thought was to save Mathilde. I didn't even think that I might need a way out."

"So, we're still trapped here?" another trainee asked.

Deborah didn't answer at first. Eventually, she said, "I need some time to think, to formulate a plan."

Arec said, "Just don't leave us. Please. We're sitting ducks. We heard the command go out into all of hell. Anyone near you dies."

"I won't let that happen," she said. Then she thought of the Elder Shadow. Deborah tried to protect him, and Malak came up from behind and killed the Elder Shadow when Deborah wasn't looking.

A sense of dread came over her. She needed to find Mathilde, but now she had over 30 trainees that would have to be with her every second she was in hell. How was she to look for Mathilde and protect this group?

A young, female trainee approached Deborah. The girl looked to be around the same age as Mathilde. "What about if we hitch rides? Mathilde told me how she would do that when she snuck out of Levea to see where the Guardians and Elder Shadows would go.

She'd step into a shadow made by their clothing and hitch a ride. They probably didn't even realize she was doing it."

Deborah smiled at the girl. "You're right. She's the one who helped me try it out. I hitched a ride on Tor to see where he was going. It works."

"Everyone just hitched a ride on me and Keil," Arec said, pointing to the other young man. "Not only did it work, I didn't feel the weight of you at all. If I hadn't known you were there, I wouldn't have known."

"Thank you," Deborah said to the young girl and to Arec. "Thank you both for reminding me that there are ways to work this out. We'll find Guardians going into the mortal realm, and you can jump on board."

The young trainee smiled hopefully. "So, we're getting out of hell?"

Deborah rested her hand on the girl's shoulder. "That's exactly what we're going to do."

14

TOR

Tor needed to do something, go somewhere, anything. Watching his father be so broken was too much for him to handle. He hiked from one dark path to another, climbing and descending. His thoughts gave way to grief, and he stopped his trek to close his eyes and give in to it. Before he realized what was happening, a tear formed, and then another. He covered his face and in the darkness of an empty pathway, he finally released all the built-up emotion he'd been keeping under a lid.

Tears were useless in hell, and Drakkon saw them as weakness. Tor learned early in his life to bottle up any human emotion. Now, vivid memories of Drakkon's torture flitted through his brain. His grief was palpable. All he had ever wanted was to be loved, to be nurtured. Instead, he was beat down until he had barely any humanity. It wasn't until Marcy—beautiful, complicated Marcy— that he began to feel again. And now, she was gone. Tor's mother was dead, and his father was so broken Tor didn't know what to do to help put the pieces together again.

Feeling depleted, he thought of the crystal spring. Maybe a good dunking was exactly what he needed. Immediately he felt a cooler temperature on his skin. He dropped his hands and saw he stood at the edge of the cold spring. Tor's mouth fell open, then turned into a grin. Had he teleported? A laugh escaped his lips. To make sure, he thought of his private chamber where he slept. He felt the familiar tingle that took place every time he traveled through teleportation. In the blink of an eye, he stood in his private chamber. Another laugh escaped.

"Tor? Is that you?" Timothy looked into Tor's chamber. "There you are. I wanted to thank you for...why are you smiling?"

"Can't I smile?"

"It doesn't happen too often is all. So, why are you smiling? I'd like to smile too."

"Because I can do this." Tor materialized behind his father and tapped him on the shoulder.

Timothy's eyes got big, and then he grinned. "Will you look at that? Can I do it too? Like with the water?"

"I don't know. Try thinking about somewhere else you want to be, and then see what happens." Tor watched his father close his eyes and concentrate. After a few minutes, Tor said, "Maybe it'll come to you eventually."

"That's all right. I'm happy you're happy."

"Well, I wouldn't say I'm entirely happy, but with this, I'm feeling better than before. Now I must find my clothes. I'm tired of walking around naked. Teleporting will definitely help me find them."

"Samson said you shouldn't be using fire."

"Why? Why would I get this power only not to use it? I'm in a holy sanctuary, so if the Creator didn't want me to have it, then I wouldn't have it."

"That makes sense."

"Samson said there is such a thing as righteous fire. I want to access that."

"How?"

"I don't know, but this is a start. Now where would he keep my clothes. He can't burn them because they don't disintegrate, which means he's hiding them."

"I have an idea," Timothy said, snapping his fingers. "You're connected to Samson. I bet there's a way for you to access his memories. You should already know where he put them."

"True." Tor tried to concentrate and focus on where Samson put the clothes. Several scenes flashed into Tor's brain, but the one that kept repeating itself was Samson at the top of the snow-covered mountain, staring off into the distance. Sighing, he opened his eyes. "I'm not getting much."

Lin approached them. "Hello, your evening meal is ready."

Timothy smiled. "Thank you. How is your village? Are things under control?"

"Samson was able to help, but there is still unrest. It is as if the devils know where we are hiding. There's this dark foreboding that does not sit well." Lin visibly shuddered. "I am thankful for Samson. He helps protect us, but he has been preoccupied lately."

"Do you know where he put my clothes?" Tor asked. "My real clothes. I could be of more help if I had clothes that didn't disintegrate at the flick of a flame."

"All I know is that they're out of the sanctuary."

"That makes sense," Timothy said to Tor. "You can't leave the sanctuary, so he places them in the one place you can't go."

"At the mountain's peak?" Tor asked quietly. Lin's expression said everything. "That's why it kept coming up in my memories. He placed them there." Without another thought, he turned to his father and said, "I'll be back in a minute."

Tor already had the location from the memory. He dematerialized before Timothy or Lin could talk him out of it.

Tor felt the cold immediately. The mountain's pinnacle was breathtaking, but the frigid wind reminded him to find his clothes and quickly. Still, he took a moment and tried to move the clouds. "Come on," he whispered, moving his hands up and out. The clouds parted, and the sun warmed the landscape. He grinned. "Yes!"

He searched the narrow terrain, using fire balls to melt the snow. There were only so many places it could be, and Tor had run out of places to look.

"Looking for these?"

Tor froze in place. Drakkon's voice raised the hair on Tor's neck. Feeling more confident now that his powers had been restored, Tor slowly turned around to face his enemy. Drakkon held out a set of folded pants and vest. Tor remembered the last time they were together when Drakkon nearly took his life. His frown deepened, and he crossed his arms. "There's got to be somewhere else you need to be. Last I checked, there's a war coming with your name on it."

"Yes, I have been busy. But I was in the area. Kraal led me to the sanctuary where you are hiding."

"Of course, he did," Tor scoffed. "I really don't like that guy. Almost as much as I despise you. Now if you don't mind, those belong to me."

"What irony! You want to wear hell's clothing so that you can aid the light-bearers and their army."

"They are mine. I fought the three-headed beast and captured its breath for you to make them for me. It was either that or run around hell naked."

Drakkon shrugged. "Details, details. And for the record, I didn't need the beast's captured breath. You needed to work for it, that's all. Consider it training."

"I couldn't have been older than thirteen!"

"Yes, and you were successful. But that still doesn't change the fact that I gave you these clothes, so I have every right to take them back. Now if you'll excuse me, I have an unexpected guest in my kingdom, and I must check in on her."

Before Drakkon finished his words, Tor teleported to Drakkon and grabbed the clothes. "I'll take those."

But Drakkon must have anticipated it because he yanked Tor to him, pressing a poisoned knife against Tor's throat. "Cute trick. I taught it to you."

Tor grinned. "Yep, and you taught me this one too." He dematerialized from Drakkon's grip and back into the sanctuary.

"You found them," Timothy said.

"Yep, and I had a visitor," Tor said grimly. "Drakkon knows I'm here. Thanks to Kraal."

"Drakkon?" Lin said with a whimper. "As in the evil one? No wonder my village has no rest."

"He's gone. He had to go check on someone."

Timothy didn't seem convinced. "He's here for you."

"I'm safe. I'm back in the sanctuary, and he can't enter here. But I need to have a talk with Kraal. I have a feeling he shouldn't be in here."

15

KRAAL

He wasn't expecting the fight. When Samson unsheathed his sword and approached him, Kraal immediately stepped into a shadow.

"No," Samson said. "No hellish tactics in this sanctuary, and no more hiding. You must fight for your place here. And you must kill the evil seed inside of you, or you must leave."

Kraal left the shadow, still warily eyeing the sword. "My skills are not for fighting. They're for hiding and mind manipulation. If I can't use those, then you will most assuredly win."

Samson gave a slight smile. "That's sort of the point."

"So then, why fight?"

Samson deftly lunged and swung his sword. "You have a decision to make. Who do you serve?" Without thinking, Kraal dematerialized into another shadow. "Stop being a coward and answer the question!" Samson roared.

"I don't even have a weapon!" Kraal moved through shadows until he was behind Samson. He jumped onto him and wrapped his thin arms around Samson's thick neck. "How is this a fair fight when you don't properly equip me."

Samson threw Kraal off him. Kraal hit the ground hard, feeling something crack. He howled in pain. "Here," Samson said, sliding the sword to Kraal. "You now have a weapon. Get up and fight."

What had Kraal signed up for? "I don't want to fight you," he said breathlessly. One of his ribs screamed in pain. "I'm going to lose. I thought this was a sanctuary."

"You have an evil seed in you that must die."

"Then kill it and be done. I am no match for you."

"Killing the seed means killing you."

"Then how does Tor still live?"

"Because he was chosen to be reborn. If you answer correctly, you too will be reborn without the evil seed inside of you."

Kraal set the sword down and extended his arms. "Just kill the evil seed already. I don't want it anymore. I've never wanted it."

Samson furrowed his eyebrows in apparent confusion. "You don't want to fight? Michael told me that Tor fought with all his strength before finally surrendering."

"I'm not Tor. I want to be free, and if that means killing what's inside of me so that I have a chance at freedom, then death can't come soon enough."

Samson nodded his head. "So be it." Suddenly, he froze. "No. Tor, no."

Kraal was confused. "What's going on?"

Suddenly, Tor materialized in front of Kraal, completely consumed by fire. "You," he said menacingly. "You killed my mother." He lifted his hand and threw fire at Kraal.

Samson materialized in front of Kraal and blocked it. "Stop, Tor. Don't do this. You have to control your negative emotions."

"Why? This Shadow is the reason for everything that happened! He kidnapped me from loving parents. He ripped Marcy out of her life and helped rebirth her as a slave. And now? My father is a shell of the man he once was, and my mother is *dead*!" Tor shot fire out both of his hands.

If Tor had lost any of his abilities, he certainly had them back now. He expertly dodged Samson. Kraal stepped into a shadow, dodging Tor's attack. "I'm sorry," he said within the shadow's darkness. "I just wanted to be free."

"I *don't* forgive you!"

Samson tackled Tor, smashing him against the cave's floor. "How did you find your hell's apparel? I told you not to wear it."

"How do you think? With your memories. And you were too busy with Kraal to pay me any mind," Tor spat out, dematerializing from under Samson's grip.

"Stop using your hellish tactics!" Samson yelled. "They cannot be used here."

Tor materialized with a sword and swung it expertly at Samson. Kraal watched from the shadows, trembling in fear. If Samson didn't get a handle on Tor, Tor was going to kill Kraal.

Samson threw a punch so powerful that Tor flew across the cave and into the darkness beyond the cave's edge. Sighing, Samson said, "You can come out, Kraal. Let's finish this, so I can deal with Tor."

Before Kraal could say anything, Tor materialized beside Samson, bringing with him a torrent of water. It slammed into Samson, taking him by surprise. But Samson recovered quickly materializing next to Tor and putting him in a head lock.

"Enough!" the voice boomed like a shock of electricity.

Kraal stumbled out of a shadow, and Samson and Tor both shoved off each other. Michael stood amid the chaos, his hands on his hips. "Great," Tor said sarcastically.

"What are you doing?" Michael asked in accusation. "You cannot use hellish devices in a holy sanctuary."

"Why are you yelling at me like I'm some child?" Then Tor pointed at Kraal. "He was hiding in the shadows. Isn't that hellish devices?"

"He still has his evil seed inside of him. You don't." Michael approached Tor. "But every time you use these tactics, you are compromising yourself, and you're compromising our sanctuaries."

"Incredible." Tor shook his head. "This shadow slave can ruin my life, and he gets to escape? And I just have to deal with it? My mother is dead. He doesn't deserve a second chance."

Michael leaned toward Tor, his face like stone. "And neither did you. How many mortals are dead because of your storms? How many *mothers* have you killed?"

"You know what?" Tor looked from Michael to Samson to Kraal. "I don't need this. And I don't need any of you."

Kraal saw the anguish on Tor's face. It was easy to see the anger, but the anguish was heart-breaking. "He's right," Kraal said. "I don't deserve to live. Tor would have never killed all those mortals if he hadn't been kidnapped. Truth be told, he was following Drakkon's orders. Everything is my fault."

"See?" Tor said. "Even the Shadow gets it."

"Tor has made some great progress," Samson said to Michael. "But seeing Kraal here in the sanctuary is definitely having him relapse, especially since it's evident he now has his powers. But there is still hope for him."

"But at what cost?" Michael asked Samson. When Samson didn't answer, Michael turned his attention to Tor and Kraal. "You both need to leave. You are not welcome in any sanctuary until you learn to forgive yourselves and each other. Because of your actions, sanctuary defenses have been compromised. And now I know why."

"We're compromised?" Samson asked, as if it were news to him.

"Yes, that's why I am here. I'm traveling to all the sanctuaries to warn them of the compromise. An unrepentant demon infiltrated the sanctuary in Ireland."

"How'd that happen?" Kraal asked.

"I wasn't exactly repentant when I first came into the sanctuary," Tor said. "So what? Eli still beat the crap out of me and shoved his sword in my heart."

"Yes, because he saw your desire to be free from Drakkon's hold. You desired a second chance. This demon didn't. It pretended to be Mathilde. We speculate it was to get to Deborah, or it might have been to see if infiltration could be done. Now that hell knows it can be, there is nothing stopping them from trying it again."

"Anyone with a brain knows that the demon wanted Marcy—or Deborah—or whatever other name she has!" Tor was becoming more upset, and his flames intensified.

"Cool it with the flames," Michael warned.

Tor closed his eyes and breathed deeply. The flames disappeared, but he still opened his eyes, glared at Kraal, and said, "For the record, we're not finished."

Kraal nervously darted his eyes to Michael and Samson. He said, "I agree with Tor. About the demon coming for Marcy. He was there for her. Drakkon knows that Marcy will do anything to protect her family, and like it or not, Shadows are her family."

Tor's expression changed to worry. "Drakkon told me that he had an unexpected guest, and he needed to check up on her."

Kraal could see that Michael and Samson understood what Tor meant, but Kraal didn't. Not wanting to push Tor, he quietly asked, "Who are you talking about?"

Tor wouldn't look at Kraal. Instead, he kept his attention on Michael and Samson. "Where is Marcy?" he asked them. "Is it true what Drakkon said?"

Kraal turned to each person, but no one had their attention on him. "Drakkon has Marcy?"

"You shouldn't have been out there," Samson said to Tor. "Now Drakkon knows exactly where you're at. And with the sanctuaries compromised, you may not be as safe as you were."

"I'm fine," Tor said. "I'm here, aren't I? Give me some credit."

"The last time you faced him, you nearly died," Michael said.

"Yes, and last time I had no powers. But all of my powers are back. All of them." When no one said anything, Tor added, "Why would all my powers come back? If they were truly hellish devices, why show up again? Why wouldn't the light inside of me give me other powers?"

Timothy entered the room, waved at Michael, but approached Tor. "I have an answer. The powers are *yours*. Not hell's. The same with Shadows. They are powerful because they are born that way. Hell has manipulated your powers for its purposes." Timothy looked to Michael. "Every good gift comes from above. Is that not what the holy writ says?"

Michael darted his eyes and stayed quiet.

"That's why I can use my powers in these holy sanctuaries." Tor's eyes widened as revelation hit. "Drakkon never gave me these powers. He trained me and pushed me to develop whatever powers I already had."

"This may be true," Michael finally said. "But it doesn't change the fact that somehow our sanctuary became compromised. And now Deborah is gone."

No one said anything for a moment. Kraal felt fear grip him. "Where'd she go?" When no one answered him, he pressed, "Where did she go?"

"She's in hell," Michael said. For the first time, he didn't behave so put together. "There was a conflict, and she defeated the infiltrator and other demons who swarmed her. Last we know, she tried to communicate with someone from hell and used the blue mist as a portal."

"She would have been looking for a Shadow," Kraal said. "And if she's in hell, then there's a reason. Mathilde."

"Does she have the ability to move through realms?" Tor asked. "I never saw her open a portal."

"She can't," Michael said grimly. "She is technically a lightbearer, not an archangel. She moves between sanctuaries, the holy city, and the mortal realm. There's never been a reason for a lightbearer to go into hell without me leading the way."

"So, she's stuck there? Why don't you go break down hell's gates?" Tor asked Michael. "Why are you still here?"

"There is nothing I would enjoy more than to rip apart hell's gates and help Deborah." Michael glared at Tor. "But I have other orders. I need to prepare heaven's army because a war is coming.

And this time, it's different. She went into hell as a light-bearer. No one can touch her."

"But without help, she'll be stuck there," Tor said in disbelief. This did not seem like Michael at all. Michael would do whatever necessary to protect his love.

"That's what Drakkon wants," Kraal agreed. "He told me he wanted her to watch everyone she cares about die."

"I was hoping you could go and help her," Michael said to Tor.

Kraal stared at the archangel in disbelief. He noticed that Tor and Samson were now studying Michael closely. "Michael would never do that," Kraal said quietly. "He would never put Tor back into hell."

Samson moved quickly, unsheathing his sword, and pinning Michael to the ground. "Do you know what's interesting about an archangel?" He asked Tor and Kraal. Then he shoved his sword into Michael's heart. "You can't kill them."

Michael's form shifted into one of the lizard creatures from hell before turning into ash.

Samson put his sword away, but his attention stayed on the pile of ash. "Something terrible is happening," he said quietly.

"Is Michael okay? The real Michael?" Kraal asked.

"Of course. He's untouchable, but this creature knew exactly what to say. He fooled me, and I'm not easily fooled."

"He fooled me too," Tor said. "At least until he said that he wasn't going to tear down hell's gates to get Marcy."

"Is what he said about Marcy true? Is she in hell?" Kraal asked, feeling the despair land squarely on his shoulders. *Would there ever be a reprieve from hell?*

"Drakkon told me that there was an unexpected visitor in hell. I think it may be true," Tor answered Kraal.

"Yes," Samson agreed, then looked at Tor. "And they want you there."

"That creature just waltzed right into the sanctuary?" Timothy asked. "How is that possible?"

"I was distracted by Tor's attack against Kraal," Samson said. "I know about the infiltration at Eli's sanctuary, and it was this same type of creature. This makes me wonder if their disguises also temporarily allow them entry into the sanctuaries. Thankfully, they do not know where most of the sanctuaries are located."

"Is Michael going to help Marcy? There isn't a way out of hell without the power to use the blue mist." Kraal was trying not to panic, but he wasn't successful. He felt guilt and swallowed hard. After Marcy and Tor had escaped hell, Kraal had felt a certain relief. The burden of what he had done had somehow been lifted. But if Marcy was back in hell, then the burden fell squarely on Kraal's shoulders again. "This is not good. It's my fault. All of it."

"We know," Tor said coldly.

"This creature knew what to say. How did he know that Michael was rounding up the troops?" Samson shook his head.

"Michael's going to help Marcy, right?" Kraal saw Samson briefly shake his head.

"She isn't Marcy," Samson explained. "She's Deborah. Trust me, she is quite capable of handling herself in hell."

Kraal covered his mouth with his hand as if to keep the panic from coming out. He thought of the baby years earlier and of how his actions changed everything. "I need to help her," he said. "I have to fix what I've done." Glancing at Tor, he took in a breath and asked, "Would you go with me?"

16

DEBORAH

"So, does everyone understand the plan?" Deborah searched each of the trainee faces, looking for any trepidation or hesitation. But they boldly looked back at her and nodded. "The Guardian lair is our best chance at passing through a blue mist. They come and go often enough. But no matter what, do not step out of a shadow. If you get to the mortal realm without us, stay there, and I will eventually find you. Stay hidden and away from any demon or human. Got it?"

"We'll be in the mortal realm alone?" a young trainee asked. She reminded Deborah of Mathilde but with darker hair.

"This is only if something unexpected happens. Trust me, the mortal realm is safer for you than here. If you stay hidden in a shadow, you should be fine. And I'll stop at nothing to find you and get you to safety." Deborah thought of the lizard-man who shapeshifted into her resemblance. "Listen," she said quietly. "There are creatures from hell that we've never experienced. One of them can shapeshift into someone else. I saw with my own eyes. So, be careful. Don't assume it's me. Ask questions that only I would know, or if you're truly unsure, shove a sword through me. I won't die, but the shapeshifter will."

Some of their expressions wavered, but most quickly recovered. "We want to be free," Arec whispered to the others. "We can do this."

The trainees murmured in agreement.

Deborah would have never had trepidation. She would have been fearless and not given a second thought to facing evil and pouncing on it. But now, after her time as Marcy, she felt some worry for the trainees. She was indestructible, but they weren't. Not that they had any real choice. Staying in hell would kill them. Their only option was to try to get to the mortal realm. "Let's go," she said decisively.

As the trainees formed a line to step into the shadows again of Arec and Dimitri, Deborah heard the flap of wings coming from behind them. She also heard the moaning of lost souls and knew exactly who it was. She whirled around just as the monstrous Rakye opened his mouth to devour one of the younger trainees. She lunged at the demon who had tried to devour her when she was Marcy and used that anger to attack him. With a solid blow to his chest, Rakye spiraled into the air. He laughed, regained control, and flew toward her. "I've been waiting for you," he snarled.

She didn't even respond. Instead, she flew toward him and right when he reached to grab her with his talons, Deborah unsheathed her sword and plunged it where his demon heart would be. He turned to ash, and all the souls held captive within him, wailed together as they swarmed her, looking for another home. She hated to doom them, but they were already dead, and they wouldn't stop until they found something or someone to possess. Using the same sword, she started slicing through the air, cutting through the thick fog of lost souls.

Screams filled her ears, but she soon realized that they weren't coming from the souls who were nearly gone. She finished the task and looked down at the trainees. They were all running in terror as black snakes completely covered Arec and Dimitri.

"Help!" The trainees screamed in panic.

Deborah landed beside the boys and blasted the snakes off of them. "Get by me!" She yelled at the trainees. "I can't protect you if you're far away!"

But the panic had set in, and the trainees weren't listening. For a brief moment, Deborah missed Michael horribly. He wouldn't even hesitate. He'd have already had the Shadow kids out of hell and free. But he wasn't here, so Deborah shook off the doubt and moved quickly. She grabbed Arec and Dimitri. "Hold on," she ordered. She flew to one group and told them to jump into their shadows. "Hurry!"

Eventually everyone was back to hiding within the shadows of the boys' clothing. She stayed in air, searching the area for any more demonic creatures.

"He's going to kill us off one by one, isn't he?" Arec asked, a slight tremble in his voice.

"Not if I have anything to do with it." Thinking fast, she flew to the waterfall and followed it through many levels until she heard the arguing and sword fighting of the Guardians' lair.

"They're going to see you!" the other said. "You stand out like a flashlight in a dark night."

"Don't worry," she said, even though her words were clipped and short. "I could kill them all. We just need to find a way out of here, and these brutes are our best bet."

But there were many of them. Monstrous soldiers of the underworld. Led by Drakkon himself but leaders in their own right. They were the masters of the Shadows. Ruthless, dangerous murderers. They abused the Shadows, forcing them to do Drakkon's bidding or suffer a fiery fate.

Michael had disguised himself well as Lynde, a Master Guardian who was as fierce as he was gruesome. Then Deborah thought of Tor. He had stood out from the mass of ugly Guardians, but he had been just as lethal, if not more so. How many times had he tried to kill her? The only reason she wasn't dead is because the immortality of being a light-bearer hadn't gone away even while housed in the human shell of Marcy. Still, she didn't think angrily of Tor. If anything, there was an unmistakable longing that nearly rose to the surface every time she thought of him. But she shoved it down and focused on the task at hand. Getting these trainees out of hell.

A poisoned arrow whizzed by her ear, then a massive fireball, bringing Deborah back to her current dilemma. She had been spotted. But they weren't trying to shoot at her, she quickly realized. They were aiming for the two trainees. More arrows and javelins shot past them. She expertly ducked and swerved. But she wasn't exactly used to having two nearly grown men hanging on her arms.

A group of Guardians alerted others. Deborah watched as the news spread quickly. A massive Guardian army formed, all taking aim at the trainees with her. If they killed one, the whole person would disintegrate, including any trainee hiding within their shadows. Groaning, she flew to the ground. "I've got to land to protect you. As soon as we touch down, get behind. My forcefield will cover you."

"It can't cover us in the air?"

But Deborah didn't answer. She couldn't dodge the flying weapons and concentrate enough to project her shield. Landing, she instinctively pushed the two boys behind her but doing so cost her valuable seconds. Guardians didn't waste time.

They were on her, clawing, swinging, and throwing fire, some trying to rip her apart limb-from-limb. Her fighting response kicked in and she shot energy from within her, knocking them all down like bowling pins. She grabbed their swords and in a fury like she'd never possessed, she attacked the Guardians one-by-one. They fought, but they were no match for the light within her. One after another they fell, some dying by their own blades, expertly wielded by Deborah.

She paused long enough to survey the damage. But she heard their approaching steps and shouts of anger and knew another wave was coming. Deborah quickly moved toward where she had left the two Shadow trainees, so focused on the fight that she had left them alone. "Please let them be okay," she prayed, flying toward them.

She half-expected and dreaded seeing piles of ash, but both young men stood clutching each other, both pairs of eyes squeezed shut. Her energy shield clearly created a dome around them. "Arec!" she called, grinning. "You can open your eyes. Just don't move."

When he did, he dropped his hands from his friend's shoulders. "How are we alive?"

"I pushed my light onto you, but you can't move. Stay in this spot until I can get us out of here."

The other guy with his eyes now opened, said, "Uh, there's a bunch of Guardians running toward us."

Deborah turned and braced herself. How was she going to get one of them to open a portal to the mortal realm. They couldn't help her if she killed them all. Suddenly, she felt a cold chill in the air. Her hair stood on end. She turned slowly. Something else was here.

"Marcy!"

Deborah froze at the sound of Mathilde's voice. "Mathilde!" she cried. "Where are you?"

"Marcy! Help!" the girl sobbed.

The Guardians had begun their assault, so she shot them back and flew straight up, once again searching the area. "Mathilde!"

The cold intensified, which was a strange feeling in hell. But this wasn't a mortal cold, but a terror-inducing freeze. It was then she saw the two trainees, nearly blue. Her shield wasn't protecting them from the frost. But Guardians seemed unfazed, throwing fireballs at the trainees, and swiping at them with their swords. Her shield easily protected them, but how long would they last? She needed to get them out of the Guardian lair, but not without a way out.

"Marcy! Please!"

Deborah's heart nearly ripped in her chest because she understood the manipulation Drakkon was using. To save the trainees, she'd have to ignore Mathilde's voice. If she pursued Mathilde, the trainees would be in constant danger. She knew what she had to do.

Before she could do anything else, she needed to get this group of trainees to safety. But the thought of leaving hell to save the others while Mathilde suffered broke Deborah's heart. She shook her head and whispered to her friend, "I'm coming back for you, don't worry."

17

TOR

"I'm not going anywhere with you." Tor scowled at Kraal and left the room. He didn't want anyone to see the worry on his face at the thought of Marcy being back in hell.

What was she doing? He thought, but he knew. It's what he loved about her. Her capacity for empathy. Who else would forgive a tortured soul like Tor who had tried to kill her twice? He remembered when he had tried to incinerate her with fire. He thought he had killed her then. He even went back to Drakkon to report on his success. But she hadn't died, and somehow, she found a way into his spiritually dead heart. She had revived him in so many ways.

If he went back to hell, he would be playing right into Drakkon's hands. So, why was he contemplating it?

Tor knew the answer. He knew it wasn't only because his powers had returned and then some. He knew it wasn't only because he had the ability to travel between realms and that's exactly what Marcy needed. The real answer was that he missed her. And now, as chance or fate would have it, he could actually help her instead of the other way around.

But he also knew why he shouldn't go and help. He was not protected outside the sanctuary. Stepping back into hell meant quick or even worse, torturous death. He was human, and Marcy was now Deborah. She was invincible, and he was not. But he couldn't stop thinking about her in hell. She needed help. If Michael was busy securing the sanctuaries, who would go?

He heard Samson approach. Tor didn't turn to look at him. Just continued staring down the long, dark passageway that led to the outside. Even from this spot, he could feel the occasional cold wind move through.

Neither said anything for some time. Tor fought an internal war, and Samson stayed still just out of Tor's line of vision. But in the stillness, Tor felt Samson's understanding. The light bearer wasn't going to stop him. "You would go," Tor said simply, not turning around. "You would go and fight."

"Yes."

"The difference is you are a light-bearer and cannot die."

"True. I did die, but now I am immortal."

"If I go back," Tor paused, not wanting to say the location. "If I go back to *that place*, I'm as good as dead."

"There's a high probability."

"And with my past, I'm not too sure that I want to face after death just yet. I'm not too sure I'd be a light-bearer. Chances are I'd be in eternal torment."

"Only God knows. But just the same, the prophecy is that you are alive in human form. Dying would be bad for mankind. They need you."

"Even with my powers restored, I am only one person and a human at that. There are several ways that I could be killed, and that's if Drakkon doesn't torture me first."

"All of this is true." Now Samson paused, "But I understand why you feel the need to go. Love is powerful."

"Yes, it is," Tor said with a sigh. "I thought coming here away from her would help, but those feelings don't go away."

"No, they don't. It's difficult when who you love isn't the right one for you."

"But she is. She's right for me in every way. I'm the one not right for her."

"And Drakkon will use your love of Deborah to his advantage."

Tor didn't refute Samson's statements. There was no hiding his feelings for her. He tried to give them distance. He tried to stay hidden, but none of that diminished his love for her. So, instead he said, "I know. Trust me, I know. I am well-accustomed to Drakkon's manipulations."

Another moment of silence before Samson said, "I still think you can win."

Tor slowly turned to Samson and raised his eyebrows. "Against the prince of darkness?"

Samson nodded. "Yes. Tor, you are the only person who I've had to give it my all to fight. The power from the Most High that was bestowed upon me when I was a man is upon you. It must have happened when you took the vow, agreeing to the covenant. You are much more than what you were while being one of Drakkon's soldiers."

"I thought you were taking it easy on me. I had to use water to surprise you."

"No, I wasn't. I was angry that you broke the rules and found your hellish clothes. Not to mention, I was angry that you were trying to kill Kraal. Trust me, I did not hold back with you. And you not only handled it, you fought me back...hard."

Tor studied his hands. Could it be true? Thinking back on it, Tor had expertly fought Samson. And then there was his encounter with Drakkon. "Drakkon met me where my clothes were hidden. He tried to kill me, but I outsmarted him."

"What you said earlier resonated with me. You have all these giftings. None of them are from hell. They all come from God. That's why they've all manifested here in the sanctuary."

"So, now you want me to leave the sanctuary?" Tor cocked his head to the side. "Are you trying to get me killed?"

"I learned quickly that ordering you around doesn't work."

"I've been ordered around my entire life. I'm not a fan." Thinking about the impostor, Tor said, "It's apparent that I'm wanted back in hell. Drakkon pulled up some bottom dwellers to trick me into leaving. That's a major red flag. That means he's got something in the works."

"What was that lizard creature?"

"They are a sect of the fallen angels chained in outer darkness."

"The ones thrown in the bottomless pit?"

"Yes, which doesn't make sense. How did they get out?"

"That's how it knew how to sound and act like Michael. It knows him," Samson said it more to himself than to Tor.

"In all my years in hell, I've never encountered the fallen angels. Other than Drakkon. That was one area of hell I refused to go near. Once you fall in, there's no getting out."

Understanding lit Samson's countenance. "They're not lizards.

They look that way because they've been in such darkness for so long that their skin has withered and scaled."

"Do they have the strength of Michael?"

"I don't think so, and they are not indestructible either. I easily killed it."

"How does an angel go from eternal to killable? Even fallen angels should still be unable to die."

Samson shook his head. "That was part of their punishment. They used their shapeshifting abilities to come into the mortal realm and mate with women. Their punishment was to be stripped of their angelic duties and cast into the endless pit of darkness. The Most High must have stripped them of invincibility too."

"Great. So, I'm not just up against Drakkon, but also a bunch of fallen angels who can shift into anyone they'd like." Tor sighed again and turned to stare down the passageway. The situation was daunting at minimum and most likely a suicide mission.

"After I had been captured, the enemies showed no mercy," Samson said. "They plucked out my eyes, abused me in horrific ways, and kept me in chains with the largest one around my neck like a dog. I begged God for one more chance to destroy the enemy. I didn't even care that it would take my life. I just wanted them off the face of the earth."

"That's not super encouraging," Tor said. "Am I supposed to embrace death? Well, I don't. I only just met my father. I only just got out of hell. I'd like to try to live a normal life. It's as if I'll never be free from Drakkon. The moment I was taken from my parents, my life has been nothing but a nightmare."

"Then I suppose that it is truly a dilemma. Your chance at freedom is here in the sanctuary. Rational thought would say to never set foot in the enemy's territory again. Then again, love's not rational."

Tor continued to mull over what to do. Of course, he would help Marcy, but he understood that doing so would most likely lead to death. Supernatural strength was great, but there was no killing Drakkon. "There has to be a way to defeat him," Tor said. "Why can demons be killed but not Drakkon?"

"Demons aren't killed." Michael approached them.

Samson grabbed his sword, while Tor summoned fire.

"Go for it," he said. "It won't kill me." Michael reached Tor and put his hand right in the fire ball.

Samson put his sword away. "It's good to see you, brother. The real you."

Michael nodded, a grim expression on his face. "These are unprecedented times, but I am glad that you were quickly able to identify the impostor."

"It even had a similar glow," Tor said. "It was only when it said that it wouldn't save Marcy that I started to suspect."

Michael frowned, his turmoil apparent. "That is why I'm here."

"You are going after Marcy," Tor said the words, but instead of feeling relief, he felt that twinge of longing again. He might not want to die, but for a moment, the thought of seeing Marcy brought anticipation.

"No, I'm not." Michael acted pained as he said the words. "This is your fight, not mine."

Tor suddenly felt chills shoot up his spine at the words. He looked from Michael to Samson. "What was that? Did you two feel like an electrical current shot through you?"

"That's called confirmation," Samson explained. "When truth is spoken, the light within you acknowledges it. What Michael just shared is a powerful truth. That is why you felt what you did. The light is agreeing with Michael."

Tor studied Michael. "You'd have already been there, wouldn't you?"

"As soon as I found out, I was on my way to tear through hell's gates. But I was stopped."

"And you just obey? This is Marcy we're talking about."

"No, that's the thing. *You're* talking about Marcy. *I'm* talking about Deborah."

"Okay, but last time, you disguised yourself to save her. How is this time different? If you were to go as who you are, you would be in and out of there in seconds."

"Last time, I wasn't only there for her. I was there for you. I needed to make sure that you two found each other. Who do you think put it in Drakkon's head to have you train her?"

"Fine. But now, she's back in there without a way out."

"She has a way out," Michael said. "*You.* Last time, she went to save you. This time, you're to go and save her."

"I can't believe my ears. So, one minute I'm not to leave the sanctuary, and now, plans have changed, and I must go into hell itself."

"Things are different. We weren't expecting you to have all your powers, plus you have Samson's strength. Now we can see that all of this was to prepare you for your purpose. And getting Deborah out of hell and helping free the Shadows is a part of it."

Once again, Tor felt the electrical current surge up his spine.

Michael stepped closer to Tor. "Last time Deborah went to hell to save you, I was in there for twenty mortal years. All my angelic duties were put on hold because of my love for her. And I would do it again, but this time, there is someone else who loves her just as much as I do. I trust you, Tor, to do what you must to get her out."

"But Drakkon will my use my love for her to manipulate me. You can't die, but I can. What you are asking is for me to sacrifice myself for her because that is exactly what will happen."

"I don't think so. If you were going to your death, I'd find some other way. What I do know is that Drakkon underestimates you. You are strong, Tor, and you are an incredible fighter."

Tor's mind went in several different directions. He wanted nothing more than to see Marcy and help her, but he couldn't pretend this was anything more than a death sentence. As if trying to convince himself, he said, "I go, get her out, and come right back. Maybe no one has to know I'm there. If I leave from here, I can grab her and come right back to the sanctuary. That could work, right?"

"Well, not dressed like that," Samson said. "You can't wear hell's clothes anymore. You are not on their team."

"Listen, if you think I'm going into hell without using fire, you are wrong. Also, wouldn't it help me blend in? That could work in my favor."

"You are not going to blend in," Michael said, agreeing with Samson. "You have the same aura from the light that we have. You'll stand out no matter what. You're one of us now."

Tor was surprised by the warm affection he felt. It wasn't like he ever had friends. Still, he mentally shook himself and said, "I get what you're saying, but I can't wear human clothing. I tend to burn the material quite frequently."

"We have a better idea," Samson said with a grin. To Michael, he said, "I'm going to take Tor for a bit. We'll be back."

"Sounds good. I'm going to find Kraal. We need to have a conversation."

Samson raised his eyebrows at Tor and said, "Follow me," then disappeared in front of him.

Smiling, Tor said good-bye to Michael, connected to Samson's thoughts, found him, and teleported to the same location outside at the top of the mountain. Samson stood with his back to Tor, facing the panoramic view that spanned as far as the eye could see. "I'll never get use to this view."

"It's hard to appreciate it when I'm going to die of frostbite," Tor said through chattering teeth.

"That's right." Samson turned to face him. "It's nice not having to worry about weather conditions. Follow me."

Tor followed Samson as he moved a large boulder just slightly. "Reach down where the stone lay. You'll find what you're looking for. I'll hold this in place."

While Samson kept the mammoth rock in place, Tor knelt down and found a deep pocket that contained a variety of supplies and weapons. "I don't see anything that resembles the clothing you're wearing." He moved items as he searched. "Nothing's here. Do you think Drakkon stole it? He was holding this outfit. Maybe he found it and took it."

"He wouldn't be able to access this supply chest, only light-bearers can. Besides, I didn't hide your clothes here. They were in one of the closets in the sanctuary."

Tor sat back on his heels and frowned at Samson. "Then how did he find my clothes?"

"Are you sure those are yours?"

Tor looked down and scrutinized the fabric. It looked the same, but he wasn't sure of anything. "I want out of these," he said, feeling his skin crawl.

"Then find what you're looking for. It's in there. Waiting for you." Samson adjusted his position holding the boulder in place. "Not being pushy, but this is getting a little uncomfortable, even for me."

Tor stopped listening. He felt sick. Drakkon had tricked him. He thought he had beat Drakkon, but no, the prince of darkness wanted him to have the outfit. Why? With the frigid temperature, Tor could no longer feel his fingers, and his whole-body shook. But he couldn't risk fire and burning all these supplies. "Please," he whispered, not even realizing the prayer was on his lips. "Please show me what I'm looking for."

"Tor."

But he ignored Samson. He was pushing items out of the way, searching the dark space, his head so far into the space that his aura provided the lighting. But nothing was there. Nothing that resembled clothes.

"Tor."

He sat up again and whipped his head back to glare at Samson. "What? If you could stop interrupting me that would be great. I'm freezing and can't find it with you bothering me."

Samson nodded toward Tor. "Look. You found it."

Tor looked down and froze, but this time, it wasn't because of the cold. He wore a dark bronzed jacket, already buttoned with what appeared to be actual gold buttons. The sleeves had intricate gold vines weaved somehow into the fabric. Yet, it felt light and breathable. He stood up and saw he wore similar pants as what he had worn earlier, but the gold thread had been woven through the dark trousers all the way down to what looked to be rust-colored military boots with gold tips and gold laces. "What..." but his words failed him. He eventually looked over at Samson with his mouth hanging open. He had noticed the gold thread woven through Samson's outfit when he first arrived, but he had been too preoccupied to give it much thought.

"You are now fitted as a true warrior for the Most High. This material is completely indestructible. Not only will it not disintegrate, but it protects you from any weapon. As the holy writ says, 'No weapon formed against you will prosper.'"

Once again, Tor felt the powerful electrical current shoot up his spine. "A powerful truth," he barely whispered.

Samson grinned and agreed. "Yes. It is quite a powerful truth." He patted Tor's shoulder. "Now you are ready to go and retrieve Deborah."

Feeling the rush of power surge through him gave Tor exactly the reminder he needed that he was no longer the same. He could step back into hell and get Marcy out of there. Without talking himself out of it, he reached out and summoned the blue mist. But it was no longer blue; it was red.

Tor dropped his hand and raised his eyebrows. "Red mist? Am I missing something?"

"I don't have this ability," Samson said. "I can't be positive, but it seems that the color may have changed because you switched sides."

Tor tried again. Sure enough, it was red. "Red like fire," he said. "It fits me." Then, without wasting another second, he stepped through it.

18

KRAAL

Kraal sat cross-legged against a jagged wall just outside of the training room or whatever the place was called where he was supposed to die. The evil seed inside him needed to be gone, but he wasn't too thrilled about the pain he'd probably experience. And just when he came to terms with it, in comes Tor looking to murder him for real.

He heard footsteps approach. "Hello," he said to Michael before he saw him. There was a definite aura around light-bearers and angels that set them apart from anything else. Kraal had sensed his presence when he first entered the cave. But once again, something felt off.

"I wanted to check in and see how things were going," the archangel said.

Kraal studied Michael closely. This one didn't have a powerful aura coming from him. Was this another impostor? *Keep cool,* he thought to himself. He nonchalantly scooted closer to a shadow. He needed to be ready. "I'm surprised to see you," he finally said. "I wouldn't think you could take a break from your responsibilities to check up on me."

"And Timothy. I'm here to check in on both of you." Michael returned Kraal's gaze. And Kraal knew. This wasn't Michael. His eyes weren't his. Kraal swallowed, realizing that he was in serious danger. With Samson busy with Tor, he was left with this creature. His nerves on edge, he began to ramble. "Well, I freed myself and made it to the sanctuary only to be attacked by Tor and then told that Marcy is back in hell. Not that I'm surprised in either case, but it's been a lot. I don't know if I should stay here or go and help her. I asked Tor to go with me, but he turned me down." Kraal looked away.

"A lot is going on." Michael sat on the ground beside Kraal. His massive build seemed to dwarf Kraal when sitting side-by-side. Every part of the mammoth archangel looked like the real Michael. So much so that Kraal started to second-guess himself. But no, something wasn't right. "I'm also here to check on Tor's father. Where is Timothy?"

Kraal's insides trembled. What would this creature want with Timothy? He was an innocent human. But Kraal already knew the answer. Drakkon would want Timothy to get to Tor. "I-I don't know."

"I think you do," Michael said quietly. "I think you know where he is, and I think you are going to take me to him." When Kraal didn't answer right away, Michael frowned. "You're doubting me. Why would I hurt Timothy?"

"Michael wouldn't, but we both know you're not him." Kraal didn't waste another second. He didn't care if it was a hellish tactic, he scooted into the available shadow and dematerialized.

Michael—or his impostor—acted unphased. "You are denying the inevitable. I will find Timothy, and I will report your refusal to help me. When the time comes, you will die a horrible death. Now, if you excuse me, I have no more time."

"Kraal?" Timothy called out from inside the training room. "Kraal? Can I have a word?"

Michael's impostor smiled in Kraal's direction. "That was easy enough," he whispered. "I didn't have to subject myself to talking to a filthy Shadow after all." He left Kraal hiding in the dark and walked into the training room. "There you are," he said to Timothy. "I was looking for you."

"Michael!" Timothy said in relief. "You are a sight for sore eyes. It has been intense these last few—"

Kraal heard a body fall to the floor. No! He brought his hands to his mouth. *Go!* He yelled internally. *Help him! That's Tor's father!* But Kraal didn't move. Terror kept him frozen in the deep recesses of the shadow.

By the time Samson found Kraal, it was too late. "Kraal? What happened? I got here as fast as I could."

Kraal stayed crouched in the shadow. "He took Timothy."

"Step out, please. There is no need to be afraid. Not in this place."

Those words jolted Kraal out from the shadow. He stepped out and said, "No need to be afraid? One of Drakkon's demons literally just walked in here and took Timothy! And he said that I was going to pay for not helping him. Those are both very good reasons to be afraid."

"Another Michael look-alike. Interesting strategy. Our defenses would be down because we had just killed one."

"And it sounded like Drakkon wanted Tor to help the trainees. Like this is all a part of his plan!"

"Stop it!" Samson said firmly. "Stop cowering to the evil one. Don't you understand yet that his manipulations only go so far? God has the ultimate say. Period."

"He walked out with Timothy, if the poor man's even alive! Did God plan that?" Kraal was yelling, but all the pent-up emotion inside of him needed an outlet. "Why does it have to be like this? Why can't we live in peace? Why?"

Samson sighed. "We'll continue the conversation in a minute. I'm going to see if I can find the impostor." Samson disappeared in front of Kraal.

WHEN SAMSON RETURNED Kraal was heaving for the third time. "I couldn't save Timothy," Kraal said before gagging again into an old pottery jar.

Samson shook his head. "I'll be throwing that away."

Kraal snapped his head up and scrutinized Samson. "How do I know you're not an impostor?"

Samson rolled his eyes. "You know it's me. Just like you knew the others were impostors before anyone else. You have the gift of discernment. Don't deny it."

"I wasn't sure it was an impostor." Kraal did question the weird sensation he felt when he first saw the impostors, but he didn't say anything. Why hadn't he?

"You doubted yourself because your eyes saw Michael."

"If it's really you then why are you making Tor go? Why aren't you helping him?"

Samson frowned. "It is not my fight. Oh, how I wish it were, but it's not. I'm stationed here as Guardian of this sanctuary."

"As soon as Tor gets there, Drakkon will be waiting."

"Drakkon won't know what hit him. Give Tor some credit. He's a force to contend with. And if you already know that this would be his demise, why did you ask him to go with you?"

Kraal looked away; the guilt apparent. "It's hard to explain."

"No, it's not. You just don't want to say the truth."

"I don't know what you're talking about." Kraal still couldn't meet Samson's gaze.

"You still have the evil seed inside you. It is battling your desire for goodness. You can't help it. One part of you wants to save Deborah and the Shadow trainees, and the other part of you wants to be there when Drakkon captures Tor so that you can bask in his approval."

Kraal felt the darkness. It agreed with Samson. It also wanted Kraal to attack him, but the Shadow resisted. No. He wanted goodness. He wanted freedom. "I need to get this evil seed out of me. Please."

"I don't know if there's time. The war is nearly upon us, and the work is great. Your healing process will be long and extenuating. It's a lot for me to process."

"You? I'm the one who has to die, remember?" Kraal swallowed the lump in his throat. "What part do I play in any of this?

Other than I'm the one who got us all in this mess in the first place."

"Listen, I don't have a lot of answers, but somehow you and Tor and Deborah are all interconnected. And now, Tor needs you. He has gone to help retrieve Deborah."

"Then let's get on with it. Cut out the evil, and I'll go and help."

"You understand what happens once the evil seed is gone?"

"I'll be in a lot of pain? Yes, but I don't want to go back into hell if I still have the evil seed inside of me. What choice do I have?"

"Did you see Tor when Deborah and Michael were fighting the onslaught of demons? In the graveyard? I thought you were there." Samson seemed perplexed.

"Yes, I was there." Kraal looked away guiltily. "I was there to trick Marcy."

"So, then you saw how Tor nearly died?" Samson asked. "He nearly died because he had been stripped of all his powers. He was just a human."

Kraal started to put the puzzle pieces together. "If the evil seed comes out of me, will I lose my powers?"

"Yes," Samson said. "You become fully human. Then with proper training, your powers will be restored based on the divine's purpose for your life. With Tor, they all came back and then some."

"But it takes time," Kraal added, finally understanding. "Time we don't have. If you kill the evil seed inside me right now, I won't have the necessary skills to help anyone reach safety."

"Yes," Samson said simply. "That's why I'm perplexed. I need to go pray and think. The path will be shown to us."

Kraal studied his hands for a moment. His internal struggle was driving him mad. One minute he wanted to extract revenge on everyone, and then he felt guilty and wanted to help everyone to freedom. He knew he would not be able to help if he had any remnant of evil in him. "If I have evil in me, I will be no good to Tor's rescue efforts. Any way we look at this, the evil in me has to die."

Samson nodded. "You're right.

"Then let's stop talking about it and get it done."

19

DEBORAH

The onslaught of Guardians turned to a full-on demonic attack. Deborah's fighting was a bit distracted because she was constantly checking the trainees to make sure her protection shield still enveloped them. She needed to get one Guardian to open a portal, but they were too busy trying to kill the trainees. From snakes to three-headed creatures, she dizzyingly slashed and hit and pulverized anything that got in her way or came near the kids.

"Enough!" Drakkon's voice commanded, and his minions immediately obeyed. "What are you doing?" he hissed at Deborah. "You broke our agreement. How many of my soldiers have you slaughtered?"

"I told you that I wouldn't hurt anything unless they attacked first. And they did. All of them. You know it, so cut the charade of indignation."

Drakkon surveyed the dwindled number of his hellish troops.

"You come to my kingdom, and you start a war? Oh Marcy, you are going to wish you hadn't have done that."

But Deborah's attention was redirected to a red mist opening beside the trainees, she nearly shot through the air to protect them until she saw Tor step through. The panic was immediate.

What was he doing? Why would he come back? He's supposed to be safe! If Drakkon spots him, he's dead. Deborah nearly groaned at the thought of another human to protect. She was barely protecting the trainees!

But Tor didn't even look her way. He wasted no time motioning for them to follow him. He was helping!

"Sir," a Guardian called out in alarm. "Sir, it's Tor."

"Do not interrupt me," Drakkon commanded. Still, he turned to where the Guardian pointed. But Tor and the red mist were gone, along with three of the trainees. Would Drakkon notice the trainees missing? Drakkon turned back to Deborah. "As I was saying, because of your actions, your little friend is going to die, and since all of the Guardians have been ordered not to release you," Drakkon approached her and whispered vehemently, "You get to watch her die."

Righteous anger roared through Deborah. "I'm done with your games. I'm done with you. Now give me Mathilde, or I will kill every demon in hell. And regardless of what you say about me being only a light-bearer and not as big or as strong as Michael, we both know that you can't touch me."

"I'm not going to touch you," he said. "What I'm going to do is hold you captive. You are not going anywhere. Ever. No one will help you escape. Even your betrothed, the illustrious Michael, has been commissioned elsewhere. Let's just say I'm keeping the angelic armies busy."

"Like you stand a chance." Deborah shook her head. A small part of her—the part that was Marcy for 20 years—felt the fear, but Deborah knew better. She knew that Drakkon's threats meant nothing, and that eventually Michael would find her. And that's if she couldn't find a way out herself. She had a feeling that she would be out sooner than Drakkon anticipated. "Now, I'll ask again. Where is Mathilde?"

"Sir!" the Guardian bellowed again. "It's Tor!"

This time Drakkon was quicker and spun around fast. Tor paused just long enough to lock eyes with Drakkon, smirk, and wink. Then he stepped through the red mist and disappeared. While Deborah had chatted with Drakkon, Tor had incredibly got every trainee out of hell.

"Follow his path and slaughter them all!" Drakkon spun to face Deborah. "You think you've won? You've won nothing! Tor is exactly where I need him to be to die. Since he's no longer hiding in your precious sanctuary, he's fair game."

"Don't I have say in this?" Tor asked, stepping out of the red mist and next to Deborah.

Deborah wasted no time, immediately projected her shield around Tor. The Guardians charged and Drakkon lunged, but Tor grabbed Deborah's waist and stepped through the red mist and onto the top of a frozen mountain.

The trainees all huddled together, shivering. But Deborah felt such relief at being out of hell that she threw her arms around Tor. "Thank you," she whispered. "And what's with the red mist? It's no longer blue."

Before Tor could respond, Samson approached. "Hello, Deborah."

Deborah released Tor who had not reciprocated the hug. "Samson!" She threw her arms around the giant man who easily picked her up and embraced her. He too seemed reserved. She noticed he was not looking at her. His attention was on Tor.

"What happened?" Tor asked Samson. "You are blocking me from seeing something. What is it?"

"Did you take the Nazarite vow?" Deborah asked, but she already knew the answer. Of course, Tor would take the vow, which would connect him to Samson and any other he made the pact with.

Samson appeared as if he might cry. "It's Timothy. He's gone."

"Stop blocking what happened! I deserve to know so that I can fix it."

Samson released a breath, and his gaze bore into Tor's. Understanding illuminated Tor's face and then anger. "Where is Kraal? I'm going to kill him." Tor disappeared before anyone could respond.

Deborah turned to Samson. "I take it Tor got all his power back."

"And then some."

"He went in and out of hell like it was nothing." Deborah still couldn't believe that they were out of there. "Let's get these trainees into the sanctuary."

"Not here," Samson said. "You know that. They'd have to swear to the Nazarite vow, and with Kraal here, I'm now training three. I don't have the authorization."

"I understand that, but there are outer chambers of the caves that the trainees can stay to get warm and be semi-protected until we figure out what to do. All of this is new to us, but we've got to provide some shelter at the moment." She glanced over at the trainees who were huddled together and shivering.

"Fine. Take them inside. I've got to handle Tor, and we need to figure out what happened to Timothy."

Samson disappeared before Deborah could ask what happened to Timothy. But the pained expression on his face told her it wasn't good. "We'll have to do what we've done before," she said to the trainees. "Step into shadows from Arec and Dimitri's clothes and hurry. We're too exposed out here." She grabbed the two young men's hands and immediately placed a protective shield around them while the trainees pushed to have first dibs into the shadows of their clothing. Deborah itched to get them into the tunnels of the caves where there would be shelter and some warmth. She told herself it had nothing to do with Tor. But she couldn't lie not to anyone, including herself. Now that she saw him, her overprotectiveness had kicked into overdrive. How was he doing? Why did he leave?

She flew up into the frigid air, telling the two young men to hold on for a few more minutes. Even though this wasn't her sanctuary to protect, all light-bearers knew every inch of each other's dwelling places. It was part of the heavenly host protocol. Now, she understood why.

Once she found an opening, she flew inside and through a maze of tunnels. Eventually she dropped them off just outside the sanctuary's perimeters. The trainees poured out of the shadows and began to rub their arms and legs. "I need you all to stay here. You're protected by my shield in case anything comes after you."

"We'll make it easy and just stay in the shadows. Not even

Drakkon can touch us there," Arec said, then found a shadow to step into. With the glow of the sanctuary pushing back the darkness of the tunnels, there were more than enough shadows for everyone to hide.

"I don't know how long I'll be but stay hidden." Deborah left them and stepped past the sanctuary's threshold. The power of the Most High rushed through her, and she stood and took it in. Hell was completely void of anything good or from God, and Deborah felt like a parched wanderer taking in a long, cool drink of heavenly water.

Noise from somewhere deep in the caves stopped her from basking in the glory any longer. Metal crashed against walls, something hard slammed against the ground. Deborah flew through the cave tunnels to what appeared to be a large training area.

"Don't try and stop me!" Tor roared, completely engulfed in flames.

Samson flicked him off like he would a flea, smashing Tor against a wall. "Killing Kraal is not going to help you find your father."

Kraal? Deborah scanned the area, searching the shadows. Kraal was good, but she easily sensed where he was hiding. "Kraal, step out from the shadow and answer questions," she said, walking past Samson and Tor to where Kraal hid.

He materialized in front of Deborah. "You are all right," he said with a breath of relief. "That is good news indeed."

Tor lunged for him, but Deborah was quicker. He stopped himself before plowing into her. "Get out of my way," he said in a low voice.

"You need to calm down," she said. "Samson is right. If Kraal has information, taking your anger out onto him isn't going to help. I thought you were trained as a light-bearer. We have no place for vengeance."

"Oh, so you too have forgotten that I was raised and tortured in hell. Pardon me that I haven't embraced all the light-bearer rules."

"I had nothing to do with that impostor taking Timothy," Kraal said from behind Deborah's back.

She easily projected a protection shield around him. Samson came over and nodded in approval. "Thank you, Deborah. Now that Kraal cannot be killed by Mr. Angry Man, we can figure out who took Timothy and where they went."

"Kraal is once again responsible for separating me from Timothy. Excuse me that I'd like for him to learn a lesson." Tor had yet to extinguish his flames.

"What could I have done? The creature looked like Michael again. And when he asked for Timothy, I didn't give him any location. I stepped into a shadow."

"Like a coward," Tor said through gritted teeth. "I know you have mind manipulation tactics. Why didn't you try that? Even if it can't work on the impostor, you could have used telekinesis to warn Timothy."

Deborah noticed Kraal furrowed his eyebrows and frowned. "I didn't think of that," he said. "I was terrified. I couldn't think at all. I-I'm sorry."

Tor didn't act pleased. Before he said anything more, Samson stopped him. "Tor, you are connected to your father through the covenant. You need to take a deep breath and relax so that you can channel him and see where he is."

Deborah watched as Tor closed his eyes and took deep breaths.

The flames disappeared, and he brought his hands to his face, covering the emotion. "I need to be alone," he said quietly, then disappeared in front of them.

Samson too appeared grief-stricken. "Wherever they took him, it's not going to be good."

"He cares deeply for him," Deborah said, moved by the sorrow on Tor's face before he left them.

"Yes," Kraal said. "Their bond is strong. A father and son. Now separated again. The first time was my fault, but this time was not my fault. Still, I feel responsible."

"Then we will find him and bring him back to Tor." Deborah rested her hand on Kraal's shoulder. "All is not lost, my friend."

"I'm not your friend." Kraal pulled away from her touch. "If not for me, we wouldn't be in this mess. All of this is because I kidnapped a newborn baby. All of it."

"We cannot change the past," Deborah said, even though she has thought the same thing many times before. "All we can do is learn from it and move forward."

"Exactly. But what do I do? I cower in a shadow! Tor's right. I let that impostor take Timothy."

"Your entire existence has been being told what to do. Kraal, you can't expect to change overnight. When conflict arises, most Shadows cower. We were trained to manipulate minds and alter dreams, not go head-to-head with a fallen angel who could and would obliterate you in seconds. Give yourself a break." Deborah glanced at Samson. "I'll be right back. I'm going to check on Tor."

"I don't think that's a good idea. Maybe I should go instead."

Deborah sighed. "I realize that he doesn't want to see me, and I respect that, but I can get through to him. Besides, he was assigned to me, and last I checked, the assignment hasn't been revoked. Plus, it's high time you kill the evil seed still inside of Kraal. He's already been in the sanctuary too long as it is."

Samson nodded. "True."

Deborah closed her eyes and felt for Tor's vibrations. She didn't have the covenant connection that Samson had with him, but holy sanctuaries were her specialty. All the light-bearers assigned to these posts were ultra-sensitive to heartbeats, irregular breathing, and just about anything that slightly altered the atmosphere. "He's by water."

"He likes the little alcove with the clear stream and crystal stalactites that surround it."

"Got it." Deborah flew through the tunnels, following the water stream to the alcove. She slowed when she spotted Tor on his knees at the water's edge, his hands covering his face as his chest heaved from the sobs. Deborah couldn't move. She had never seen Tor cry. She had never seen him in such an emotional state. It moved her deeply. She found it beautiful and a reminder of just how human Tor was.

He stopped crying and wiped his eyes. "I said I need to be alone." When Deborah didn't respond, he disappeared from the water's edge and materialized directly in front of her. "Especially you. You need to go."

"Tor," Deborah began to speak, only to pause. What could she say? The only words that came were, "You left without a good-bye."

Tor laughed humorlessly and shook his head. "Add that to my list of sins. Now if you'll excuse me, I'm going to find my father."

"No!" She reached out to grab his arm, but he had already dematerialized. *"No!"* But he was gone.

She took a deep breath and tried to focus on where he went, but it was too far away. Wherever he went, he was definitely out of the sanctuary. Deborah felt that familiar tug of panic and knew if she was going to help Tor this time, she was going to do it the right way.

She soared high into the air, but she did not pause to enjoy the view. Instead, she called out to Michael. Here in the heavens, the call was much clearer. The noise of the mortal realm was distant. He'd hear her, and he'd come. And she needed to talk to him. Because this time she would make decisions the right way. With wise and loving counsel.

Thunder rumbled across the sky, moving toward her with precision and purpose. *He gathered the armies*, she thought. But, of course, he would. One doesn't just send fallen angels into holy places and not bring about a host of consequences.

"Deborah." Michael reached out to her, and she embraced him.

"I know you're busy," she said, not yet releasing him. "But I needed you."

"I'm here." He pulled back enough to study her. "What are you doing in this area of mountains? Or should I ask, how did you find out about Tor's location?"

She took a deep breath, pulled away, and unsheathed her sword. "Do you trust me?"

He watched her for a moment before nodding. "Always."

Still, Deborah paused. A legion of angels surrounded them, waiting for an order from their commander. This was Michael. She knew it, but she also had to be sure. As if helping her with her decision, Michael brought his arms out and said, "Go ahead."

She swallowed then lunged. The sword hit his armor and reverberated. Deborah steadied it then put it away. "There are more impostors. It's been unnerving for Eli and now Samson. You have been impersonated a couple of times already."

"I'd say I'm flattered, but I'm not. It angers me. Drakkon has unleashed chaos by releasing the fallen angels. They received their judgement. It is not for him to break the rules."

"How many are there? And how can they walk away from their eternal punishment?"

"It was a third of heaven, so legions upon legions. I don't think that they've all been released. That would be impossible for Drakkon to accomplish such a feat."

"How is it impossible?"

"They are only able to leave the abyss in exchange for another life. But only for a short time. Then all those touched by the outer darkness will be completely destroyed."

The energy inside Deborah acknowledged the truth of Michael's words. "Everyone touched by it? So, those souls who have been thrown in there to replace the fallen angels? Is their fate sealed?"

"Not yet, but you must act quickly."

"This is my battle, then?"

Michael frowned yet nodded. "I'm sorry, my love, but yes. I have been commissioned to gather the angelic armies and strike soon. Hell and all that is in it will be destroyed."

"Who is in the abyss?" She thought of Tor and covered her mouth. "Timothy? Mathilde?"

"More. It's most likely Shadows and trainees. The Shadows Drakkon didn't immediately kill, he must have thrown them there, which has allowed him to bring back those fallen angels from the days of chaos."

"But I already killed one. Does that mean that a Shadow must stay?"

"Or another soul."

"That's where Tor went," Deborah said in dismay. "He went to save his father."

"He will no doubt sacrifice himself for Timothy, which is exactly what Drakkon wanted."

"My instinct was to go immediately and follow him, but I needed to do it right this time. You are not just my betrothed, but you are wise and a warrior. How do I go about doing this? I need to protect Tor, save Mathilde and all the other Shadows." Deborah took a breath. "The Marcy in me is trying hard not to panic. But I can't mess this up again."

Michael gave Deborah a tender smile. "You are wise and a warrior too," he said. "There isn't merely a *Marcy* or *Deborah* in you. It's you. *All you.* Everything you are feeling, there is no need to feel bad or upset about any of it. If anything, being in hell for over twenty mortal years opened your eyes and reminded you that there are individuals worth fighting for and that there is a common enemy to fight against."

"I felt surer before. Now I'm questioning everything."

"Until you were assigned to protect the child, you had been

stationed as protector of the garden sanctuary. There was peace in the heavenlies. Give yourself some credit."

"Give myself credit? We are in this mess because I didn't get to the baby in time. I lost him. Then I made a decision that rocked all the realms."

"True. Before you were Marcy, you made a rash decision to infiltrate hell and save the human child. But it was brave, and it was divinely purposed. And now, with all your past experiences, you are thinking things through before acting. That shows grit and strength and wisdom."

Deborah looked away. "I just came from hell after throwing myself in there...again. Tor, of all people, had to save *me*. Go figure. I didn't realize that I had no way out of hell when I crashed their party. It was still a rash decision, but at least this time, it wasn't on purpose."

"I heard. And I heard that you were like a wrecking ball, wreaking some major damage."

Deborah shrugged, but she also let a smile escape. "They didn't know what hit them."

Michael took her hand. "I think we can come up with a plan that rescues those Drakkon has kidnapped and gets them out of hell for good."

"What are you thinking?"

"I'm thinking that it's time I distract Drakkon." Michael smiled mischievously at Deborah. "He's bringing his armies outside the holy garden, demanding an audience with the Most High. Let's just say, I'm going to be keeping Drakkon and his demons busy for a little bit."

"Which gives me time to rescue those in the abyss." Deborah felt a glimmer of hope. "This could work."

Michael nodded. "It will work. You are going to go in and finish the job. So, are you in?"

A plan started forming in Deborah's mind. "Oh yeah, I'm in."

2 0

TOR

Tor materialized behind a small hut in the local village. Hell's creatures were waiting for him. He could feel it. Drakkon must have stationed them here. Lin hadn't been lying. Poor girl. Still, he had no time to deal with regret over not believing her. Just like he had no time to grapple with the influx of feelings that came upon him when seeing Marcy again. No time for any of that. His father needed him.

He stayed hidden while watching the locals traverse the main road. Hidden among them were more than Drakkon's minions. There were several fallen angels, impostors ready to pounce when the time was right. Now that he knew what to look for, he could see the slight shimmer of illusion as they walked among the mortals. Tor's heartbeat clamored in his chest. The energy bubbled up inside him as if desiring nothing more than to zap them into oblivion. Tor closed his eyes and took a calming breath. *Don't lose your cool.* The sanctuary was in trouble, but Tor couldn't think about that just yet. He needed to find his father.

He already knew that Timothy was in hell. His tormented cries were shaking Tor to his core. It was the abyss. The bottomless pit where these forsaken fallen angels had been cast into. Which made Tor wonder how they got out and who let them out. If Tor didn't hurry, Timothy would be lost forever. His mind would become insane, and his life force would shrivel and die. Unlike fallen angels, Timothy couldn't be in that pit for more than a couple mortal days, maybe only hours. Unfortunately, it was the one place Drakkon had never taken Tor. He knew that if pushed in without chains holding you in place that one would literally fall for the rest of eternity. Even Drakkon didn't go near it.

Yet here these fallen angels showed up. They were walking around like they're on vacation. So, something changed. And Tor needed to figure out what before he made his grand entrance. The last thing he wanted was for both him and his father to be lost in the darkness for eternity.

So, he did the only thing he had never tried before. While at the water's edge before being interrupted by Marcy—or Deborah—whatever she wanted to call herself, he had prayed. It felt strange to do so, but he took a page out of Timothy's book and simply talked to this divine being like he would anyone else. It was a lot of pleading and crying, and there was the sentence, "Help me save my father, and I'll swear allegiance to you forever." Tor wasn't sure he did it right, but he felt better for it. And while talking to Marcy, he saw this village street in his mind. The energy buzzed in recognition, and he understood the vision to be straight from the Most High. So, the answers started here.

"Okay, what now?" he prayed quietly, talking to this entity that he had never formally met.

"I thought you could use some help." Marcy's voice came from behind, startling him.

Tor turned slowly, and just like every time he saw her, his heart skipped a beat. But the energy inside of him seemed to revolt. "I do need help," he said.

Marcy stepped closer and whispered seductively. "Then let me help."

Before the words had fully left her mouth, Tor grabbed the impostor and twisted its arm behind its back and slammed it against the hut's exterior. "You know, for having a couple thousand years to improve your game, you still suck at it. Now reveal yourself because we need to have a conversation."

The Marcy impostor gave a low laugh, making goose bumps shoot up on Tor. "I don't think we will."

Tor noticed several Marcy's stepping around the hut from the front and back, moving in on him. "You underestimate me," he said to them all, then dematerialized in front of them, taking the one with him.

He took the impostor to the mountain's peak because it was the first place that came to mind. He would have to work fast. Taking the light-infused cuffs that he had found while looking for his light-bearer outfit, he placed them on the impostor's wrists. Immediately, the illusion disappeared, and Tor stared into the hideous face of a fallen angel. "That's better. At least now you can't pretend to be something you're not. Now tell me about the abyss."

The fallen angel's appearance revolted Tor. He really did look like a lizard with scaly-dark skin and black nails and a green tongue.

But the creature refused to speak, and instead, it tried to lick Tor's face.

Tor grabbed its neck and squeezed. "I'd think twice before doing that again. Remember, you can die, and I have no problem with that happening."

"We long for it," it hissed. "Death puts us out of our misery. So, kill me."

The answer surprised Tor. He studied the creature, trying to envision what it had looked like before its fall. Had it been as magnificent as Michael, Deborah, and Samson? "What happened?" Tor's words were no longer threatening. Instead, they were merely curious. "What would make you get such a punishment?"

The fallen angel scoffed. "We listened to the wrong guy. He got his own kingdom, and we were thrown into outer darkness."

Tor thought of Drakkon. "So, why work for him now? Why do his bidding?"

"Why do you think? We're out of that pit. We're promised freedom. You of all people should understand that."

"But you are listening to the one who got you into the mess in the first place. Why believe him now?"

"We don't. We only hope to die before getting thrown back in. So, go for it. What are you waiting for?"

"How can I get to my father?"

"He's dead. Forget about him."

"He's not dead. He's chained in the same bottomless pit where you all were at."

"Exactly. He and that Shadow girl are as good as dead. You don't go into the abyss and not die. Being spirit beings, we were not so lucky."

"So, what changed? How come you die now?" Tor was trying to keep the upper hand, but he had so many questions, he couldn't help but ask more. "Why can you now die when you were angels?"

The creature's tongue kept flickering out of its mouth like it was unsure of what to do next. "We chose it. Drakkon offered to get us out, but there's no going back in. This time, we die. Our places have been taken. Now kill me."

"Your places have been taken?" Tor asked with an edge to his words. The realization hit him. "Did my father take your place?"

"The numbers cannot lie. If one comes out, one must take its place."

"Who all is in there?" Horror filled Tor. Who did Drakkon put in the abyss? There were numerous fallen angels in this area alone. "My father? He's in there? Answer me!"

"You already know the answer. We're here, which means someone else is there."

"You were once an angel. Is there anything in you that wants a chance at redemption? If so, help me. How can I get my father out?"

"I would rather die than help you. Besides, I have already given you the answer. Too bad you're too stupid to figure it out."

"Someone has to take his place? Just like he took your place?" Tor shook the creature as hard as he could. "Answer me!"

"Talk to Drakkon. I'm done here." The fallen angel stared at Tor with such contempt. He tried to shape shift into an image of Tor, but the light-bearer cuffs prevented him from doing so. He screeched loudly.

"Why are you siding with Drakkon? You know better than anyone that he is a liar."

"Because you have what I can never have!" The fallen angel

screamed the words so loudly, it was like chalk on a board. It shot chills through Tor, and the energy pushed back, ready to fight. *"You get a second chance! You get to be free!"*

Tor sighed in frustration. "This is getting me nowhere. I'm getting my father out which means I'm taking you back where you came from."

The creature screamed and writhed that it took Tor aback. Suddenly, the creature unsheathed a knife that Tor hadn't seen and lunged for Tor's chest. Tor had no time to react, but his light-bearer's apparel absorbed the attack, disintegrating the knife. Tor smiled at the creature. "I guess that didn't work out as planned."

The creature screeched again, lunging for Tor, but this time Tor anticipated the attack. He shoved it to the ground, threw the knife, and kept his knee on its back.

"Tor."

Tor turned to see Samson step up. "How much did you see?"

"Considering you are still at the sanctuary and that we're still connected by covenant, I heard and saw everything even before I got here. However, I've only been standing here for a second or two. Long enough to see the creature lunge at you."

"You were right about the light-bearer armor. It protected me from his attack."

"Yes, and I'm glad you didn't kill it. You understand what that means, right? If what he says is true, then that means that whoever took his place must stay in the abyss. A life for a life."

The gravity of the situation suddenly felt too heavy, and Tor sat on a protruding rock. "I'll throw this creature in myself because I'm getting my father out."

"I killed one," Samson said quietly. "Deborah said she did too.

We're going to have to be careful now that we know why they were released and how to get them back in."

"I've got to go. Every minute I waste is a minute I risk losing my father."

"I know, but Tor, please be careful." Samson extended his right hand. Tor clasped it. "If I could go, we could storm into hell together. There's nothing I'd like more than to destroy every demon there."

"You have quite a few demons still stationed in the village. Lin and the villagers still need you."

"Yes, more have arrived. It seems never-ending, but it will end. So, stay strong and keep the faith." Samson nodded at Tor as if giving him the go-ahead.

Tor took a deep breath, knowing what he had to do and where he had to go. He grabbed the impostor, and then with one last glance at Samson, he said good-bye and extended the red mist.

21

KRAAL

The darkness was consuming, surrounding him from every angle. He tried to catch his breath, but there seemed to be no air. And the screams. They wouldn't stop. He covered his ears, only to realize the screams came from him. When he opened his eyes, he gasped and immediately felt the searing pain in his chest.

"Go easy," Samson said, bringing him a cup of water. "Don't sit up just yet. There are some herbs in the water, which bring some pain relief."

Kraal tried to swallow, but his throat was parched. He drank thirstily. "I was screaming," he said breathlessly. "I was in darkness. It surrounded me. And it was alive like it was trying to choke the life out of me."

"You coming out of that means it did not win. If you would have succumbed to it, then you would have died with the evil seed. But here you are."

Even with the pain pulsating throughout his whole body, Kraal gave a small smile. "Here I am. It didn't win."

"You need to rest. It's important to remember that everything has been stripped from you other than your humanity. From this point on, the gifts that return to you will be for your divine purpose. But this will take time. Trust the process and mend."

"Rest? Is that what that was? It didn't feel restful."

"That's right, Shadows don't really sleep, do they?"

"Not near as much as full mortals do, but the humanity in us does require it at times. But we don't dream. Is that what I experienced? A dream? A nightmare?"

"That was more like a vision or alternate reality. But hey, I don't have all the answers." Samson offered a small smile.

"Have you heard from Marcy—I mean, Deborah—or Tor?" Kraal closed his eyes briefly, wishing he was stronger. He wanted to help them.

"They are working to retrieve Timothy and others. Do not concern yourself with that. Focus on rest and healing." Samson turned to leave.

"Don't concern myself?" Kraal tried to sit up. He glared at Samson. "It's my fault. Everything is. You know it. They know it. I know it."

"And yet everything will still work for the good."

Kraal wasn't too sure about that, but he was in too much pain to pursue the topic. Samson left, and Kraal fell back into sleep. The nightmares would jolt him awake only for him to close his eyes again and drift off.

His eyes shot open, and he became suddenly aware of the shift in atmosphere. Something was wrong. This didn't make sense because Kraal shouldn't have any of his supernatural abilities. But he felt the immediate urge to get out of the room. He tried to ignore it, telling himself that it was the nightmares that made him feel anxious. He opened his mouth to call out to Samson but stopped.

Get out.

Kraal heard the urgency of the words. He pushed himself, cringing at the pain, and forced himself to slide off the makeshift bed and onto the floor.

Get out. The voice urged.

There was nowhere in the small room to hide, and he couldn't step into a shadow anymore. He crawled to the door, sweat dripping off his forehead from the simple exertion. He wanted to stop and examine this new sensation for he had never sweated before, but that would have to wait.

As he crawled down the hall and rounded a dark corner, he heard movement behind him. Kraal peeked around the corner and saw Samson moving with a purpose, searching each room down the cave's corridor.

Get out.

Kraal crawled as fast as he could down the dark hallway. There was no light at all. Then again, why would there need to be. Samson's aura shown like a bright light everywhere he went. The same with Tor. As Kraal crawled, not knowing where he was going or if he would hit a wall or worse, he wondered if he'd ever have that light shining in him.

He heard someone a couple yards behind him. He snuck a quick glance, and there was no light that he could tell. Chills shot through him. This Samson was an impostor? And the impostor was looking for someone. It had to be him. No one else was around besides

Samson. And Drakkon had vowed to kill Kraal if he double-crossed him.

Kraal moved as fast and as quietly as he could. The darkness aided in hiding him. He made turns and crawled down corridors like he knew the place…as if something inside directed him. Whatever it was, he trusted it far more than anything he'd ever encountered in hell.

His arms trembled from fatigue. He took a turn where he saw a faint light. It was too late to turn around, and he hadn't heard the footsteps in some time. Hopefully, he had lost the impostor. To be safe, he crawled along the wall where darkness prevailed. It felt strange not to be able to step into a shadow and become invisible, but there would be no more of that.

He reached the small alcove and saw a fire lit within a small contraption that sort of resembled a human's stove…sort of. But the fire provided just enough light that Kraal soon noticed the pool of water surrounded as far up as he could see of crystals. He immediately crawled to it, desperate for a drink.

Just as he put his face near the water's surface, he heard footsteps much closer than before. Not knowing where else to hide, Kraal crawled into what was frigid waters and dunked himself, hoping the impostor wouldn't think to look into the water.

The cold took his breath away while at the same time lighting a fire inside of him. The pain of the injury immediately dissipated. The water seemed to move him away from the shallow end and far away from the edge. When Kraal came to the surface, he was at the other end of the spring where there was no natural light. Once again, he was in shadow, but not as before.

He saw Samson enter. "Kraal?"

It was him. Samson's light showed bright in the alcove, but Kraal didn't move. He felt the water push against him as if trying to keep him in the spot.

Samson turned and looked right at where Kraal hid. "Stay there," he said quietly. "Don't reveal yourself."

Before Kraal could wonder how he could hear Samson from so far away, the impostor lunged from the dark hall and onto Samson. But it was no contest. The real Samson wrestled with the impostor and in a matter of seconds, had him bound and cuffed. Whatever Samson had used shattered the illusion, and the ugly creature writhed under Samson's foot. "Give me the Shadow!" It screeched. "Give me the Shadow, and the human is yours."

"I don't make deals with the devil," Samson said coolly. "Instead, I'll deliver you back to where you came from. We'll put you back where you belong and get the human out at the same time. Sound good?"

The water released Kraal and pushed him across the spring to the water's edge. He was still hesitant to get out.

Samson's attention turned to Kraal. "Feeling better?"

Kraal nodded. "What kind of water is this?"

"Living water. One doesn't taste of it and stay the same. I neglected to tell Tor and Timothy that, but they figured it out."

The creature underneath Samson narrowed its eyes on Kraal. "Traitor," it whined while it tried to wiggle out of Samson's grasp.

Kraal desired courage to stand up to this vile fallen angel, but years upon years of being a slave kept him mute. Besides, he might be feeling a lot better, but he had no idea if he had any supernatural abilities. He was nothing more than a human. Still, when he dropped his head to gather his thoughts, he stopped at the reflection staring back at him. "My eyes...They're normal."

"No more black orbs. The abyss is no longer inside of you," Samson said.

The creature screeched again, but it was no match for Samson.

Kraal steeled himself and stepped out of the water. He reasoned with himself that he was safe with Samson in the room. "The pain's gone," he said, marveling at how good he felt. "It vanished."

"Yeah, the water is pretty powerful," Samson said absently, becoming lost in his thoughts.

After an awkward length of time, Kraal' attention turned to the creature. "We can't just kill it?"

"Not if we want to get the others out. It's a soul for a soul." Samson didn't look at Kraal.

Kraal sensed that Samson was struggling with something. Not only did he sense it, but he also *felt* it. There was this warm electricity inside of him that seemed to respond to Samson's internal struggle. Kraal studied his hands, unsure of what to make of it. He heard Tor talk of some sort of energy inside of him that was alive and helped him and warned him, communicating with him often. Is that what this was? "What are you not telling me?" Kraal eventually asked Samson.

"We have to get this creature back to the abyss." The creature whined in response, but Samson pressed harder against it, silencing the impostor.

"Do you have access to all the realms?"

"No, I'm a light-bearer like Deborah, not an archangel."

"What does that mean?"

"It means we were human once. Upon death we were given

elevated stations in the heavenly realms. But we don't leave these stations unless commanded to do so."

"Did Marcy have a station?"

"Yes, she was guardian over the holy gardens until she was called to protect the human child. I, however, have not received such a calling. My station is here, protecting this sanctuary and the people who live in the mountain communities."

Kraal tried to wrap his head around the thought that Marcy was a human before she became a human to step into hell. "This is a lot to process. But I don't understand what that has to do with us."

"Because I cannot access hell. Light-bearers have no need to do it. The archangels can, but we can't. Deborah even said as much. She was stuck in hell this last time until Tor retrieved her."

"But Michael can access it?"

"He's an archangel. He has access to all realms and kingdoms."

"So, you can't take this creature to the abyss? Let's find Michael. He can do it."

"He has his hands full. While Drakkon has been distracting us with these impostors, he has been lining up troops outside the gates of the heavenlies."

"What? How is he able to do that?" Kraal started to feel fear, but the energy didn't seem to like it. He took deep breaths. "So, he really is going for the white throne. He's always wanted it. He promised Tor that he would sit beside him and help rule."

"He's always wanted what he can never have," Samson said in disgust. "Trust me, it's not going to be pretty for Drakkon or his legions, but he's too stubborn and rebellious to back down and admit defeat."

"How long will it take? Could we put this creature somewhere until Michael is done?"

Samson shook his head. "Humans cannot be in the abyss. Drakkon is breaking many rules, and throwing the Shadows and Timothy in there is breaking the biggest rule of all. And once he loses the war, his punishment will be severe. There will be no more going to and fro between hell and other realms."

"And the Shadows will be stuck in the abyss?"

"Yes. We are racing against the clock." Samson finally looked at Kraal. "I can't leave, Kraal, but you can. You're going to have to take this creature back to the abyss."

Kraal swallowed the lump in his throat, and despite the energy bubbling up in excitement at Samson's words, his knees started knocking. "I-I don't think I can. I-I'm not strong enough. I-I'll die."

Samson frowned. "If you don't, who will?"

Kraal didn't answer, but if he was being honest with himself, he was asking the same question.

KRAAL PACED BACK and forth in his room. He'd left Samson to take care of the creature hours ago. He needed time to think. Samson told him he'd be thinking too, and that they would need to come together in the morning with a plan. Kraal had given up at one point and tried to lay down and sleep, but the energy inside was having none of that. It wouldn't let him rest. So, now he paced. "There's nothing I can do right now," he whispered to the energy. "I can't access the realms. We have to figure out a way to do it. Now, will you let me sleep?"

Suddenly, the energy boiled up inside of him, shooting through him so fast, he cried out and fell against the wall. He clenched his hands trying to stop the pulsating sensation that burned at the fingertips. It was then he noticed a small white mist on the other side of the room, reminding him of snow-like crystals. But just as fast as he noticed it, the white mist faded quickly. Was someone or something trying to step into his room from another realm? Another thought came to him: *Had that come from him?*

Unable to contain the mounting energy within, Kraal extended his hands. Energy shot out from him, and another white mist appeared. Panic manifested, and he dropped his hands. "No, no, no, no," he said, pacing again. "I don't want this. No, no, no, no, no... I cannot go back there. There has to be someone else."

"There isn't." Samson stood inside the doorway. He stared at the fading white mist with a mix of awe and curiosity. "This is incredible. Tor's turned from blue to red, and yours is white. It's uniquely yours."

"I don't want it to be incredible. I can't go back there."

"He chose you."

"Whoever he is chose the wrong guy."

"He doesn't make mistakes. You're the guy."

"No." Kraal shook his head. "Not happening."

"What about the other Shadows? And weren't you willing to go back to hell to retrieve Deborah?"

"That was different. I wanted to go with Tor. He's powerful. I'm not."

"What just happened shows that you have been gifted with the supernatural power needed to get this job done. You're it, Kraal. If you don't go, you are choosing a fate worse than death for fellow Shadows."

"Stop." Kraal kept shaking his head. "Don't try to make me feel bad." But he did feel bad. Isn't this what he had wanted? To help free the other Shadows?

"What about Timothy? Doesn't he deserve saving?"

"That's why Tor's there," Kraal said barely above a whisper. "He'll help Timothy."

"But he needs another soul to get Timothy out. You have the impostor to provide him."

Kraal's knees had yet to stop knocking. He was terrified at what Samson was saying, especially since the energy buzzed in what felt like agreement. He brought his hands to his face and tried to steady his breathing. "What's happening? This is too much, too fast. I should be recovering, not saving everyone from the abyss."

His eyes closed; Kraal focused on calming down. As his body relaxed, he was suddenly standing in the center of a village road.

Kraal blinked a couple times to stop whatever vision or reality this was. But it didn't work. He pinched himself. Nothing. All he felt was the icy wind. He wrapped his arms around himself, longing for something warm. Had he teleported? It didn't feel like he had. Then why was he in the middle of a village?

He'd seen this place before. Then it hit him. It was the same village outside this sanctuary. Now it looked war-torn. Huts had collapsed, and small buildings that had once lined the street no longer stood. *What happened here?* He thought as he started to investigate. That's when he saw the mounds of bodies littered across the debris. He felt movement behind him and turned around to see who it was. One of the creatures from the abyss moved toward him, shifting to look just like Kraal. Soon, others appeared, all resembling him. Chills ran up and down his body, and they weren't coming from the frigid temperature.

He tried to move, but he was frozen in place. As one approached, it said, "And to think, you could have saved them."

"Kraal?" Samson's voice called out to him, bringing him back to the room in the cave. "Kraal? Are you with me? Where'd you go?"

Kraal blinked and saw that Samson had grabbed his shoulders and was shaking him. "I'm here."

Samson nodded and released him. But he kept a steady gaze on Kraal. "Interesting. This is all interesting. What did you see?"

"How do you know I saw something?" Kraal couldn't look Samson in the eyes.

"There are several among us light-bearers who are given the gift of sight. These visions show us different paths."

Kraal frowned at the thought of an entire village being decimated. "They're innocent," he whispered to himself. He glanced up at Samson and saw that he patiently waited for Kraal to explain. "All of them are innocent. The villagers, and even the Shadows. None of us asked for this."

"What did you see? I can help you sort through it."

"The village here—not far from this sanctuary—destroyed. All dead. Other than the fallen angels or whatever they are. They approached me, all looking like me, and said that I could have saved them."

"The villagers? Or the Shadows?"

"I'm not sure."

"My visions are always very specific. Did you see anyone other than the impostors?"

"No, only the dead, and there were a lot of them."

"Did you get a close look at any of them?"

Kraal closed his eyes and concentrated, and suddenly, he was back in the village, taking in the carnage around him. He swallowed hard and moved closer to those scattered in the debris. A body lay face-first in the dirt outside a hut. It was a girl with dirty blond hair and a singed arm. "No," he said, already knowing who it was. He crouched and slowly turned the body. "Mathilde."

Kraal closed his eyes tight, thinking about the sanctuary. "Take me back," he said. "I don't want to see anymore."

"You're all right," Samson said, his voice bringing Kraal back to the room within the sanctuary. "You'll learn to better control them. But did you get the answer you needed?"

"It was Mathilde. Marcy's trainee. She was dead." Kraal suddenly felt a tightness in his chest and moisture leak from his eyes. He brought his hands to his face, and for the first time, he wiped away tears. "Tears," he said in amazement. To Samson, he asked, "I get to be free while they die? Mathilde dies? That isn't fair."

"It seems to me that you're the one who can stop it. If nothing else, your help is needed to change the path that has been showed to you."

Kraal slid onto the floor and rested his head against the rock wall. He was terrified, but he also knew that he couldn't let Mathilde or anyone trapped in the abyss die. Not if he could help it. "You said that visions are specific?"

"Yes, everything in it means something. Nothing is wasted in a vision."

"So, the hoards of fallen angels coming to me all with my face?"

Samson raised his eyebrows. "Yes, that means something. How many were there?"

"A lot, and they were coming up from the ground almost. Just appearing shifting into my face and moving toward me."

"And the vision was the local village here in the mountains?"

Kraal nodded. "And I felt the icy wind. It pushed against me."

"All right, now piece it together." Samson gave a smile of encouragement.

"The fallen angels are still at the village, which means this sanctuary is surrounded. But they're not here just for the sanctuary. In the vision, they were surrounding me. Coming at me from all sides."

Samson sat on the ground in front of Kraal and urged him to continue. "What else?"

"Just the village in shambles and the dead bodies everywhere. And the one person who was face-first in the debris was Mathilde."

"Why do you think the fallen angels have stationed themselves here? Why this sanctuary?"

"They're preparing for battle? Maybe they want to overtake the sanctuary and kick you out?"

"That'll never happen, and the fallen angels, of all creatures, know this. They are not here for me, and they are not here to attack the sanctuary. We weren't in your vision."

A thought crossed Kraal's mind and sent a shock of revelation through him. "They're here for me. They didn't arrive until after I was in the sanctuary."

"And why would they be here for you?"

"I-I don't know. To kill me? To get back at me for being a traitor?"

Samson leveled his gaze at Kraal and raised his eyebrows again as if the answer was already given.

But Kraal wasn't seeing the whole picture. "Why would they want me? I'm insignificant."

"Are you? What did they say to you in the vision?"

"Nothing really. One of them sarcastically said that I could have saved those who had died." Kraal stopped and stared at Samson in astonishment. "Is that why…"

Samson nodded. "I think the impostors have tried infiltrating this sanctuary for more than just Timothy. One of them interrupted your death match with me, possibly trying to stop the ritual of eliminating the evil seed. Another came not long after that and sought you out first before Timothy."

"But why didn't it take me? We had a conversation before I realized what it was."

"I don't know. Maybe it was toying with you, or maybe it was sizing you up."

Kraal had so many thoughts and emotions rolling through him, but whatever this energy was within him felt wonderful. It was warm and electrical and seemed to have a mind of its own. But the more he thought about everything, the more he knew with a certainty what he had to do. Like it or not, whether he felt worthy or capable, his help was needed. He stood up and said, "I think I know what I have to do."

22

DEBORAH

This time, Deborah stepped into hell prepared. Michael had given her several items to help capture demons and exchange them for those souls hanging in the abyss by hell's chains.

"They're chained," Michael had explained. "I'm positive. Because to be thrown in the abyss with no chains would make that soul unrecoverable."

"So, why wouldn't Drakkon just throw them in? Why chain them up at all?"

"Easy. For you. For Tor. You and Tor would just ignore him forever if he didn't have anything to hold over your head. He needs you on his turf. He feels it'll give him an edge. With Tor, it might, but it doesn't impact you at all." Michael held up his finger. "Other than, he will try to manipulate your heart. That's why you're going back there now."

"I will be as quick as I can. Go in, capture demons and exchange them for Timothy, Mathilde, and the other Shadows. I don't know how many, but I'll figure it out."

"There are numerous fallen angels stationed outside Samson's sanctuary. But I'm not sure if that's the only place they're stationed."

"One came into Eli's sanctuary disguised as Mathilde." Deborah paused and allowed herself to think about the sheer magnitude of what needed to be done. Still, she steeled herself and prepared mentally for the challenge. This was *her* fight, and she was determined to win it.

Michael glanced over his shoulder at the masses of angels waiting for him. "I wish I could go with you," he said quietly.

Deborah grabbed his hand. "We don't *wish*," she said fiercely. "We worship our Creator, and we fight for what's right, especially for those who cannot fight for themselves."

Michael nodded once. "For the Almighty."

"For the Almighty," Deborah repeated. "And for every soul who longs to be free from the enemy's grasp."

"Let it be so." Michael kissed Deborah's hand, gave it one final squeeze, and then extended his hand, opening a portal. "This is the main hive of legions of imps. If I was Tor, this is where I would be."

Now, as she searched the filthy squalor of the imp's hive, she became uneasy at how quiet it was. And empty. The imps were gone. Something was wrong. The energy within her agreed. She flew up and searched...nothing. Flying quickly to the waterfall that connected the many layers of hell, Deborah paused and momentarily considered which level to search next.

"Marcy!" Mathilde's voice shrilled in her mind. The Shadow trainee started whimpering and whining, almost like an animal.

"I'm coming," Deborah said, not knowing if her friend could hear her. Flying through level after level, she refused to focus on hell's low numbers. The demons and Guardians also were in short supply, but she attacked and captured as many as she found, using the golden cuffs fused with heaven's strength. It stripped demons of any abilities and rendered them powerless.

She needed to find Tor, but she already had an idea where he was. She didn't want to go empty-handed, knowing that a soul for a soul was the only way to free those held in chains in the abyss. "Take me to the abyss," she said to the light dwelling in her. It pushed her back to the waterfall and tugged downward. "Take these demons there, but don't throw them in yet." The demons climbed over each other to fall off the edge of the waterfall. She watched as they fell all the way into the darkness that lay at the bottom. "They just do what I tell them?" she asked. The energy responded warmly. "Where have those cuffs been all my life?" she asked as she started her descent. "They would have been helpful lots of times."

Deborah reached the darkness and remembered Michael's warnings. "Be careful," he had said. "It is an atmosphere full of evil. It will work hard to extinguish your light. It can't destroy it, but it will mess with you so that you question things, and in so doing, lessen your control of the power within you." She kept descending, and her skin began to crawl. The light within her revolted. The screams of torment hit her ears. It sounded like thousands upon thousands calling her old name.

"Marcy! Marcy! Marcy!"

Her light broke through the darkness as she flew down, making it screech and recoil at the intrusion. She pushed harder, sending waves of light energy to the surroundings. She could see a path straight down, so she kept moving.

Deborah tried to mentally shut off the screams, but it was all around her. The horror, the nightmare, the hell all attacked her with every wail. *Keep pushing,* she told herself. *You have the light of the Most High. There is nothing to fear.*

Although the energy was a bit more subdued, she still felt it pull back, telling her to slow down. Suddenly, she covered her ears. She must have been successful at shutting out the horrors because they now came at her full throttle. *Make it stop,* she said to the energy, but it didn't respond. She looked around but the darkness was a veil of black just outside her glow. It pushed against it, trying to reach her.

"Tor?" she called out, but her words came right back to her. It wasn't going to let her communicate. She hovered slowly pushing against the darkness. There was a small, waning light coming from her left. It was barely there, but against the darkness, Deborah knew it didn't belong. "Tor."

It wasn't until she was nearly upon him, that she saw who it was. He watched her with apparent relief on his face. Even though she couldn't hear him, she saw him mouth her name, Marcy. She reached out her hand to him, and he grabbed it. Suddenly, his aura strengthened and the light inside him exploded. Deborah felt the energy shoot through her as well.

"What was that?" he asked, his voice now clear above the wailing.

"Two can put a thousand to flight, three can put ten thousand to flight." Deborah added, "It's from the ancient texts. Basically, we increase in power when together."

Tor glanced down and his face fell. "He's down there. I can hear him."

"We'll get him out, Tor," she said. Deborah glanced around now that their light had successfully pierced the darkness. "I brought some demons to throw in the abyss. But I need to find them. Come with me."

With their hands still clasped together, Tor nodded. Deborah extended her energy, and Tor's feet left the thin ledge surrounding the abyss. "Stay by the ledge," he suggested. "If they haven't fallen in yet, that's where they'll be."

But Deborah didn't answer. Her attention was glued to the mammoth mouth of the never-ending darkness. "It's as big as a city," she said in horror. "I can't see where it ends."

"I tried to teleport, but I couldn't visualize what was out there. I could only stay in one place."

"Remember when I attached myself to your shadow and followed you into darkness? Is this what it was?"

"Not quite. That was the tunnel leading to the prison. It's where tormented souls go who are new to the afterlife. It's similar but not nearly this intense. Not to mention, I had an evil seed in me at that point, so I was one of them. Now I'm not, and it's driving the darkness insane. But even then, I never encountered the abyss."

The two of them stayed quiet as they stayed close to the ledge, flying just out of reach of the abyss. Deborah noticed chains attached to the ledge all dangling into the mammoth hole beneath them. If Deborah focused on it for too long, it felt as if even the screams were reaching toward their feet trying to pull them down. So, she didn't think about it. She kept her focus on exuding the light within her. "There," she said, pointing to dozens of demons littering the edge. They barked, growled, and screeched along with the tormented souls. "I'm not entirely sure what will happen if I drop one in."

"I had a fallen angel as prisoner. I threw him in as soon as I got here, hoping that the abyss would hand me Timothy."

Deborah turned to Tor. "What happened?"

"One of the chains started rattling. It was close enough that I heard it, but far enough away that I couldn't see. But I called out to Timothy, and I didn't hear anything."

"I doubt he heard you. It's like the darkness is a wall blocking communication. I couldn't call out to you. I tried, but the darkness blocked my voice from reaching you."

Tor furrowed his eyebrows. "Could you hear me? As soon as I saw your light, I started bellowing your name."

"Not at all. I saw a tiny flicker of light and figured it had to be you. There is no light in this place. Even as I came closer, I saw your mouth move, but I couldn't hear you."

"We need to go back to where I heard the chain rattle," Tor said with urgency. "Now that we have light, we can see what happened and who was released."

Deborah nodded. As she flew back the way they came, she said, "Tell me where to go."

Tor searched the ledge. "So many chains...there!"

Deborah saw the body huddled against the wall. It didn't look like a man. It looked like a girl. Before she could get too hopeful, she spotted the brown hair clumped around the girl's head. Deborah brought her and Tor to the ledge and stepped onto the ground. "Hello," she said, walking over to the girl. "We're not going to hurt you."

The girl shot her head up and over at them. It was Trina, one of the girls from Deborah's Shadow training group. "Marcy?" she barely whispered. Then she threw herself around Deborah's legs. "Marcy, save me. Please. I can't take it anymore."

Deborah crouched down and wiped Trina's hair from her face. "Yes, I'll get you out of here, but I first have to help the others."

"There are too many of us. He took some and threw them in cages over the inferno, but most of us were chained and thrown in here."

"Yes, I found the ones in the cages. They are safe now."

"Arec? Did he...make it?"

Deborah nodded and smiled. "He did. I'll get you to him as soon as I can. Have you seen Mathilde?"

Trina shook her head. "You don't see anything down there. You only feel and hear. You feel the hands reaching for you and the bites of those who've lost their mind. And you feel the darkness too. It plays with your sanity." She stifled a sob.

Deborah straightened herself and surveyed the mammoth hole. Then she turned her attention to the clifflike edge of the abyss. To Tor, she said, "You said it right...So many chains." She pointed out the chains dangling from the edge as far as their light carried.

"Let's go throw those demons in and start freeing as many as we can." Tor still had her hand. "Please. I need to get my father out of this hellhole."

Deborah doubted it would even start to be enough, but not knowing what else to say, she agreed. "Let's start there."

23

KRAAL

Kraal stood beside the chasm that he had witnessed days earlier when he had freed himself from Drakkon's poisonous shackle. It wouldn't take long for him to be noticed. If those fallen angels were looking for him, they'd catch his scent eventually. But still, Kraal didn't move. He was overwhelmed with how far he'd come from that moment. For the first time in his previously miserable life, he felt alive, and he was allowing himself to hope. Something he never did before.

He glanced down at his midsection and placed his hand on it. The energy was incredible. He was completely whole. No pain, no agony. Only strength and an overwhelming sense of peace that he was right where he needed to be. Even the trepidation he experienced in the cave had somehow dimmed.

The energy started humming within him. Kraal closed his eyes to settle it. There was definite power to whatever this light energy was. But as soon as his eyes were closed, he felt the atmosphere shift. Another vision.

He opened his eyes to darkness. Not just darkness, the darkness. But its attention wasn't on him. Its entire force seemed to be pushing against a distant light. Kraal didn't move. Even though he couldn't see around him, he sensed the great abyss before him. The wails, the sobs, the gnashing of teeth, it chilled him, but now that he understood that it was a vision, he reminded himself not to fear. Strangely enough, the energy inside him buzzed so loudly that it helped to focus on that and not the horrors around him. *Why am I here?* He asked it. *What do I need to see?*

The light approached. As it approached, Kraal noticed that he was standing next to someone. He turned his head, and his stomach dropped. "Drakkon," he whispered, only to clamp his mouth shut.

But Drakkon didn't look his way. His attention stayed focused on the light coming toward them. Drakkon had a sinister smile on his face as if anticipating something.

Kraal turned back to the approaching light, knowing that light in this dark place only came from one set of beings. That's when he saw it was Marcy and Tor. They flew with their hands intertwined. They were talking between themselves, and they had yet to see Drakkon. He then watched as Drakkon slowly stepped back letting the darkness cloak him, but not before Kraal saw the large, opened chain he had in his hands.

The cold air surrounding him cut off the vision. He opened his eyes back at the chasm in front of him outside the mountain village, only this chasm wasn't more than a large hole, and he could easily see the bottom. It had nothing on the abyss. Kraal felt the immediate urgency again. Drakkon had something planned, and from the vision, neither Tor nor Marcy seemed aware of his presence.

Kraal thought of Tor and of the way his life was forever changed because of Kraal. "I have to make it right," he said to himself. But he couldn't go without the fallen angels. They needed to be sent back to where they came from. That was his purpose. He didn't merely know it, but he felt the truth in it.

He took a deep breath and got to work. Kraal hadn't tried mind control since before his cleansing, but everything else had come back and then some, so he was taking a chance that this would work too. He remembered Samson warned him that the powers bestowed by the Most High must only be used for good, or he would be stripped of them. Samson even told him a little about his past life when his divinely ordained abilities were stripped from him due to bad decisions.

He visualized the buildings Samson had pointed out that contained numerous fallen angels. They both reasoned that only fallen angels disguised in human form would be able to be under the influence of Kraal's mind control. *Come to the chasm by the jagged rocks on the outside of town, south of the tree with the golden leaves. Find Kraal. He's waiting for you.*

Kraal moved quickly, getting in position on the other side of the chasm. Many internal voices all talked at once, making it hard for him to concentrate. Mind control meant hearing the inner dialogue. That meant there were a lot of fallen angels in this area. Kraal prayed they would be enough.

Once in position, he used his former Shadow abilities and continued to beckon to them in their minds. Kraal didn't focus on the darkness or depravity of these fallen angels' thoughts. Instead, the light within helped him focus on just what he needed to say to bring them to him and nothing more.

He felt their nearness before he saw them. When the mass of fallen angels saw him, all of them shifted from their previous form of some villager to look like Kraal. It was like a sea of Kraal faces running toward him.

Come to me, he beckoned in their minds. He wasn't sure how he was able to use these abilities on fallen angels because he couldn't on any of the real ones. Samson and he concluded that it must work when the fallen angels had shifted into a human. Doing so made their minds accessible. Whatever the reason, it was working.

Since all of them were running toward Kraal, none of them bothered to look down. Masses of the impostors fell into the large chasm not knowing what had happened. More and more kept running toward him and falling in.

He waited for the last one, keeping an eye on those at the bottom of the hole all trying to climb over each other to get to him. When the last of them were in, he saw some gaining ground and crawling on the tops of others to reach him. "Samson!" he called.

"I'm ready," Samson yelled from above him.

"Is it a big enough rock? We don't want them squished! We only need the opening covered!" Kraal yelled and pressed himself against the rock wall. A couple of the impostors were a little too close for his liking.

The cliff above him shook, and debris began to descend. He covered his head as best he could. Suddenly, a giant rock fell on top of the chasm, shaking the earth where Kraal stood. He lost his balance but quickly regained it.

Everything was eerily quiet.

Kraal reached out in front of him and touched the massive rock that resembled one of those skipping stones he'd seen when he was still dream-weaving. It was long, smooth, and flat. And the size of several rig trucks all next to each other.

"Trust me," Samson said as he climbed down the jagged edge of the cliff then landed in front of Kraal. "They are not dead. I took the diameter from the giant hole in the ground and found a nice piece of stone at the bottom of a glacial lake. That's what took me so long. I may have strength, but I still had to move this bad boy from there to here. Try taking it from fifty feet below water to the top of this jutted cliff. I almost broke a sweat."

Kraal raised his eyebrows. "Really? I didn't think that was possible."

"Nah, I'm just teasing. I enjoyed the challenge. It was quite the workout." He grinned. "Now, you need to get going. You've got some prisoners to free. This area is within my jurisdiction, so I will keep an eye on them, as well as on the Shadows that are still hiding in the cave."

For a moment, Kraal hesitated. He was about to step back into hell. Was he ready for this?

"You are ready," Samson encouraged him. "If not now, then when?"

Kraal nodded. Taking another deep breath, he extended his arm.

"Remember what we talked about," Samson said.

"I remember," Kraal answered as the white mist appeared.

TOR

Tor stood at the edge of the abyss, his eyes surveying the black hole. He could see nothing. Oh, but he could hear everything, and that nearly tormented him into madness. Especially knowing that his father was in chains and dangling inside of it.

"How long did it take after you threw in the fallen angel to hear the chain?" Marcy asked. Tor had quit trying to call her Deborah. She would forever be Marcy to him.

Having her here had brought relief to the torment. He wanted to tell her, but he didn't. Instead, he held tight to her hand, needing her light now more than ever. "Almost immediately," Tor said, a large knot already formed in his gut.

"The chains didn't move this time," Marcy said.

"How many of the demons were there?"

"Several dozen. More than enough for these chains to move."

A thought formed in Tor's mind. "A soul for a soul," he said.

Marcy turned to him, her expression mirroring his at the realization of the truth. "They don't have souls."

Just hearing her say the words brought on a wave of helplessness. "I'd throw myself in, but there's no guarantee that he'd be the one freed. I don't know what to do."

"It makes sense," Marcy kept talking. "Fallen angels have souls but not demons? I feel like I should know this."

Tor had stopped listening. There was an evil near them that sent chills through him. The whole place was evil, but something new was present. Something that hadn't been there until now. The energy seemed to boil inside him, so much so that he brought his hand to his chest. "Something's not right."

But Marcy was no longer talking. She swung around, unsheathing her sword. "Aren't you supposed to be busy waging war?" she said through her teeth.

Tor tried to turn around, but he couldn't. At least not fully. He looked down to see two large shackles slightly above his ankles. His stomach dropped. "What is going on?"

"Release him!" Marcy ordered, the terror clearly visible on her face.

"I don't think I will." Drakkon stepped beside Tor, gently pushing the sword away. Looking straight at Tor, he hissed, "You're mine. Always have been, always will be. And no amount of angelic clothing and weaponry can protect you." To the both of them, he gloated, "I knew the two of you wouldn't be able to resist saving these poor, pathetic souls. I knew you'd be back. And so now, Tor will suffer the same fate as his father, and you, my dear Marcy, get to watch."

Marcy snatched him by the neck and flung Drakkon into the

abyss. The move happened so fast that Tor had no time to react, especially when Drakkon flew out of the black hole in full dragon mode. "I have to let go of your hand," she said to Tor. "But this ends now."

She released him and flew straight for the dragon, her sword aiming for his heart. But the darkness seemed to be waiting for the moment and now pushed Tor toward the ledge. "You're mine," it screamed. "Mine..."

Tor tried to think up fire, but the terror swarmed him. The energy inside of him rumbled as if ready to fight, but Tor's mind couldn't focus on anything.

Psst. Tor. Someone whispered his name. Great, he was losing his sanity. Tor brought his hands to his ears, but the voice didn't stop calling to him. *Tor. Can you hear me? I'm coming over there. Don't do anything crazy.*

Tor lowered his hands and looked around him. Without Marcy's light, his was dim in comparison. And why could he suddenly hear someone? The darkness put a wall between him and Marcy, why would that change now? With a sigh, Tor closed his eyes, forcing himself to forget the noise and whoever was talking to him and try to get out of the chains.

Tor? If you can hear me, give me a sign.

Tor snapped his head up. Who was that? Unlike the darkness's whispers, this was clear and penetrated the darkness.

Good, so you can hear me. It's Kraal.

Tor made a face. "I don't know where you are but leave me alone!" But the words flew back at him. The darkness wasn't going to let him communicate.

I can see you trying to talk, but I don't think we can down here. I'm communicating through telepathy. And I know you don't want my help, but I'm here to give it, Tor. I'm here to redeem myself, so please let me.

Tor didn't say anything. Instead, he tried to project his thoughts. *How do you plan to do that?*

First, by getting you out of the chains.

Where are you? Did you bring special tools?

I'm across the ledge, but I'm making my way over. I'm trying to do it without falling in. And no, I don't have special tools, but I was able to break free from the shackle Drakkon had put on me. It doesn't have power over you if you don't let it.

I'm not understanding, Tor thought in frustration. *It's around my ankles. How do you not let it have power?*

Michael told me once that I was not a slave, and if I believed it, Drakkon would have no control over me. I kept saying it until I believed it, and then, the shackle fell right off. No special tools required.

Suddenly, Marcy landed right next to Tor, surprising him. "We don't have long. I punched him as hard as I could, which sent him reeling, but he'll be back once he's recovered. Now, let's get you out of these...what?"

"Kraal is here," Tor said. "He's in my head, telling me to believe these chains are going to magically fall off."

I see you talking to Marcy, Kraal's voice infiltrated his head. *You're probably saying something about me being crazy and that it'll never work. But hey, what do you have to lose? If you want to be in chains in outer darkness for all eternity, you do you. But I say give it a shot. Tell Marcy I'm almost to you.*

"It worked for him," Marcy was saying. "The shackle fell right off. No one else has ever done that before. Samson told me it was powerful and impressive."

Was it that simple? Tor studied the chain. At any moment, Drakkon would come roaring back.

Say the words, Kraal spoke to Tor. *I whispered, 'I am free,' until I believed it.*

Tor had no time to feel ridiculous. The chains needed to come off so that he could figure out a way to save his father. "I am free." The words reverberated against the darkness. Tor could see it ripple from the words.

Marcy took Tor's hand again, and he immediately felt an outpouring of energy flow through him. "Say it again," she said. "And this time, believe it."

Tor took a breath, but as he opened his mouth, a roar shook the air. Anger filled him, but this was a different anger than anything he'd ever felt. It was anger at the one who had caused so much suffering, an anger toward the one who had beaten and abused Tor for most of his life, an anger that Drakkon would dare hurt these souls stuck in the chains. "*I am free!*" he roared, and the darkness not just shook, but it shattered like shards of glass. Their light poured through the vast expanse, pushing into crevices that had never seen light before. Even the abyss had been cleared of the cloak of darkness and the masses of captives were clearly visible.

The dragon unleashed fire at them. "I will destroy you!"

Marcy moved to fly toward Drakkon, but Tor stopped her. "Stay here. We're stronger together." She nodded, then extended her protection shield as the dragon continued to spew fire at them.

"What *was* that?" she asked Tor. "You completely eliminated the powerful darkness in this place. It was incredible."

"I think it's what Samson would call a righteous anger."

Drakkon landed on the ledge, changing to his human form.

"This won't end until you die," he seethed. "So, put yourself out of your misery and just die already!"

Distract him, Kraal's voice came through loud and clear, only no one heard it but Tor. *I've got an idea.*

"You like making deals, right?" Tor's mind whirled with how to distract Drakkon. "Let's talk. We've always been able to talk about things."

Kraal's voice interrupted his thoughts: *I need you to take a couple steps back.*

Tor took a step back and then another. Sure enough, Drakkon moved closer to him. "I'm done making deals with you," Drakkon said. "The only deal I make is the one where you die."

Marcy tried to interject, but Tor squeezed her hand, stopping her. "Fine," he said to Drakkon. "I'll die, but you free my father."

"If you truly meant it, you'd release this intolerable light bearer and step out of her protection." Drakkon looked from Tor to Marcy.

Tor went to release Marcy's hand but paused at the snapping sound. All three of them—Drakkon, Marcy, and Tor—all blinked at each other for a split second surprised at the intrusive sound. Then, as if on cue, all three looked down to see two large chains around Drakkon's ankles.

Realization hit Drakkon, as he tried to shift into dragon again. Only whatever power was within the chains held him to this current form. "What is this?" he said, continuing to struggle to change forms. "What did you do? What have you done?"

"Those chains block one's power. Its why Tor couldn't utilize his power when they were on him. Well, that is until he figured out, he did not have to be captive." Kraal stepped around Drakkon and moved to Tor and Marcy. "This ledge is scary. There is barely any room to move, and then with all the chains. Talk about a hellish maze."

"You?" Drakkon asked in unbelief. "How did…"

"How did I get here? How did I hide? How did I put the master of darkness in chains? All good questions. And I don't have to answer any of them anymore because you are *not* my master."

Drakkon pressed against his chest. "Please, I don't feel right. Something's wrong." He looked at each of them, his eyes imploring. He seemed to shrivel right before their eyes.

Marcy lunged at Drakkon, grabbing him by the neck. "Your days of torment are over. Let's see how you like dangling in a never-ending pit for eternity."

The cool, stylish Drakkon had transformed into a whimpering, small man with thinning hair and rotting teeth. "P-P-Please," he stuttered. "H-Have m-mercy on me."

Tor watched as Marcy paused, feeling conflicted. "Do I need to help throw him in?" he asked exasperated. "This is the devil himself."

"She did the same thing when I asked for mercy," Kraal said quietly. "She gave it to me."

Marcy dropped the pathetic Drakkon. He fell on the ground and pulled his knees up to his chest, rocking back and forth.

Tor watched in horror and amazement. Was this the same demon who had ruled over him for years?

"You remember that day?" Marcy asked Kraal.

"All the time," he said. "I never felt right for how it all happened. I only ever wanted to be free." Kraal turned to Tor. "I'm sorry that I ruined your life."

Tor looked away, struggling with mixed emotions. He closed his eyes and tried to find his father's voice now that the darkness had broken. *Father? I'm here. I'm coming for you.*

But Tor heard nothing.

"Tor," Marcy said. "Kraal helped us beat Drakkon. We couldn't have done it without him."

Father? Talk to me. We're linked through the covenant. I need to know you're okay.

Tor strained to hear something that sounded like a muffled sob.

"Tor? Did you hear me? Kraal helped us."

"Yeah, so?" he snapped, knowing he was behaving badly but also struggling with a host of other issues. "We still have Timothy and Mathilde and all the other Shadows stuck in this pit. Forever! So, excuse me that I'm not groveling in thanksgiving."

"About that," Kraal said. "I have a surprise for both of you. It's the reason I came here. That and warning you about Drakkon."

"Warning us about Drakkon?" Marcy asked. "You knew?"

"It's a long story, and I'll tell you everything, but for now, wait here. I'll be right back." Kraal extended his hand and walked through the white mist.

Tor and Marcy exchanged shocked expressions. "What is going on?" Tor asked her. "Kraal can travel the realms?" He reached out and touched the lingering white mist. "White?"

Marcy grinned from ear to ear. "This is incredible!"

Before they could discuss Kraal's abilities, a white mist appeared right beside them. No one came out at first. Tor leaned in to investigate when suddenly a fallen angel was thrown through. It thrashed and screeched, but Tor wasted no time. He pushed it the rest of the way into the pit. A chain started moving on the other side of the abyss.

"Yes!" Tor shouted through the white mist. "Do you have any more?"

Another fallen angel was thrown from one side of the white mist to the other. Tor and Marcy got to work quickly, completing the job by shoving each fallen angel into the pit where they came from. There seemed to be a never-ending supply of the lizard-like creatures, but the sound of chains coming up made Tor so giddy, he worked without complaint until the job was done.

Hours later, the ledge surrounding the abyss was full of newly-freed captives. "We need to get them out of here and to safety," Marcy said. "It'll be easier to sort through who's who."

Tor couldn't help but search around him, but there were no signs of his father. Timothy wasn't doing good. Tor felt it profoundly.

Marcy gently touched his arm. "Tor, he's here. I can feel it. Let's get them all out of here, and we'll get them sorted."

Without a word, Tor nodded and extended his hand. "Kraal, lead the way."

Kraal acted surprised then agreed. "It'll take a while. Most are not doing well. Where should I take them?"

"Outside Eli's sanctuary," Marcy said. "They won't be able to enter without agreeing to eliminate the evil seed, but it's a good place for them to stay. We'll set up camp outside of the sacred forest."

Tor watched at Marcy and Kraal moved the Shadows from the ledge through the white mist. It was painstaking, and it nearly drove Tor crazy not to stop what he was doing and search for Timothy.

A dozen or so were ushered through the white mist, then

another dozen or so, and then another. Marcy called from the other side of the abyss. "Tor! Over here! I found her!"

Being able to see the other side helped Tor move from one point on the ledge to the other by teleportation. Once there, he saw Marcy kneeling next to Mathilde. Marcy looked up at him with tears streaming down her face. "We found her."

Tor pushed back the frustration at not finding his father and knelt on the other side of the Shadow trainee. "Hey there," he said to Mathilde. "I'm glad to see you're okay."

"I knew she'd come for me." She gave a shaky breath and rested her head in Marcy's arms.

"Get her out of here," Tor said. "I'll keep looking for my father."

"Kraal can take her," Marcy said. "I don't want to leave you."

Tor reached out for Marcy and affectionately squeezed her shoulder. "Go. The prince of darkness is nothing more than a chained imp. I'm fine."

Marcy didn't need much convincing. She helped Mathilde up, and the two of them moved through Kraal's white mist to the mortal realm.

"She'll need someone to get back here," Tor said to Kraal. "You should go and be there to help if she needs it."

"I will in a little bit," Kraal said. "I want to help find Timothy. We still have work to do here."

Tor looked at Kraal and gave a brief nod. The words, *thank you,* were on his tongue, but he held back.

The two of them moved Shadows from different parts of the ledge to one location using Tor's teleportation. This allowed him to materialize all around the ledge of the abyss and search for Timothy.

"There's a problem," Tor said when he set the last Shadow trainee down by Kraal. "There are two chains left."

There was a short cackle that made Tor's skin crawl. He turned to see that he wasn't too far from where they had left Drakkon. "Oh no," Drakkon teased. "What will you do?"

"Shut up," Tor ordered. But his anger hadn't quite calmed down. He took quick strides to Drakkon and lifted him up by his neck. "Hey Kraal, does the prince of darkness have a soul?"

Drakkon quickly changed his tune. "No, I don't. I'm a demon, an imp. I'm nothing. But I can help you get your father back. I promise. I'll sign by blood."

As Drakkon kept babbling and pleading, Kraal walked up beside Tor. He too glared at Drakkon. "Actually, Tor, I heard somewhere that Drakkon is the first of the fallen angels. I think he even went by a different name."

"Stop! Please!" Drakkon begged. "I ask for mercy. Mercy!"

"Here's the thing, Drakkon. Marcy may be a light-bearer, but I'm not." And with that, he tossed the prince of darkness over the edge of the cliff and into the abyss.

DEBORAH

She took a clean washcloth that Eli had provided and washed Mathilde's face and neck. The girl still whimpered occasionally and had yet to release Deborah's arm, hugging it tightly with the one arm not burned off. "You're safe," Deborah said to the girl. "I'm right here."

"Get it out of me. Please. I don't want any part of that darkness. Get whatever out of me that needs to set me free."

"Okay," Deborah said. "You rest right here. Let me go find Eli and see what his thoughts are."

Deborah walked past and stepped over hundreds of Shadows and Shadow trainees that had been held in chains and thrown into the abyss. Many huddled together, some cried, but most hadn't lost their minds. They acted relieved and grateful for the rescue.

She did a quick survey of the area, checking to see if any-colored mist had returned. She wasn't thrilled at the thought of leaving Tor, and now, without he or Kraal opening a portal, she had no way back. Instead of worrying, she focused on taking care of Mathilde and the others.

Moving quickly, she stepped into the sacred forest and took in a rejuvenated breath. Power surged through her, and the light inside of her pushed through her and out her fingertips.

"Better?" Eli said as he approached.

"You have no idea."

"You're right. I have never encountered hell, and I admire your strength for not only encountering it but freeing the slaves."

"It wasn't me," she said. "It really wasn't. I helped, sure, but it was Kraal. He showed up unexpectedly and saved the day."

"Are we talking about the same Shadow that had that poisonous shackle on his hand?" Eli didn't hide his surprise. "How did that happen?"

"He's changed, powerfully changed. It's incredible. His eyes are normal, and he has abilities that he never had before. He can move through realms, he somehow managed to capture a legion or more of fallen angels and dump them back in the abyss, and he locked up Drakkon."

"Wait, what?"

"He put shackles on Drakkon. He said he knew he was supposed to do it, like he knew about it beforehand."

"Was he awarded *sight*? That is truly powerful. And he's still there?"

Deborah did another quick scan of the area outside the forest. "Yes. I've been waiting for him or Tor to open another portal to send me through. I wasn't thinking straight when I saw Mathilde. I let them talk me into taking her here. I didn't even consider that I didn't have a way back."

"They'll be fine. It seems like there is a divine purpose for all of this, which means that we need to let be what needs to be."

"I'm trying, which is why I'm here. How do we go about this? Mathilde is ready to get the evil seed out of her. I won't dare to cross any of them through without a total surrender to this endeavor."

"It will be painstaking, and it would be great if I had help. Could other sanctuaries assist? We could separate them into groups."

"I can see. Should I travel and ask?" Deborah paused, not wanting to leave the situation at hand. "I should stay in case Tor or Kraal need me."

"I agree. Let's get this group comfortable and bring me Mathilde. There's no reason I can't start now with her." Eli added, "One more thing, we must offer a choice to these Shadows. They do not have to accept our help. Some may not. If they choose not to, they must leave the premises. They may not be in the sanctuary here, but they are too close to stay without desiring a true covenant and transformation."

"Absolutely," Deborah said.

Eli acted like he wanted to say something more.

"Out with it, my friend. It's not like you to hold back."

"We were so sure the prophecy was about Tor, but what if it wasn't? Kraal is definitely a human anomaly. By sheer force of his will, he broke through Drakkon's poisonous shackle. And if he's doing everything you say he is, maybe your job was to protect him, so he could be present to defeat Drakkon."

Deborah didn't say anything at first. Memories flooded her of Kraal. The first time she met him was right after he had kidnapped

Tor. When she found her voice, she said, "Tor and I didn't defeat Drakkon. It was Kraal. He was the one who told Tor how to be free of the chains, and then he hid, waiting for the opportunity to use those same shackles on Drakkon. I never would have thought to do that. But, why would the Most High put Tor and his family through that horror? There had to be another way to rescue Kraal that didn't involve kidnapping and torture in hell."

"I don't know the answer to that. Tor and Kraal are connected to you. Both are human anomalies, both care for you. If not for you, then neither would be free from hell."

Deborah's throat constricted as the emotions rose. "Thank you for saying that, Eli, but it doesn't change the fact that I couldn't protect Tor as a baby."

"But you needed Tor to bring you to Kraal."

There was no denying that Kraal had a much more integral role in the defeat of Drakkon. How would she have met him if not for Tor? Deborah had no interactions with hell. Her entire light-bearer existence had been the protection of the garden sanctuary. "Well, I need to get back to them. Unfortunately, that means waiting for one of them to open the portal."

"Someone is waiting for you," Eli said, pointing up.

"Michael," she said, now zeroing in on him. "I need to see him. Let me know if Kraal or Tor open the portal again." Deborah flew straight up until she was face-to-face with Michael. She threw her arms around him. "It was awful," she said. "And we still don't have Timothy. I have to get back."

Michael released her, acting pained. "That's why I'm here."

"What?"

"Tor is going to need you." Michael kissed her cheek, a deep sadness on his countenance. Then, he extended his arm, releasing blue mist. "You need to go to him. Now."

Deborah covered her mouth, her heart already heavy. "Timothy?" Michael didn't need to say anything because she knew. She flew through the blue mist and back to the abyss, feeling more guilty than she ever had before.

2 6

KRAAL

Kraal saw Tor's shoulders sag as the chain came up. "It's not him," Tor said with a mix of defeat and weariness.

Tor didn't even acknowledge the Shadow that had been freed. Instead, he stumbled over to the last chain that dangled.

The Shadow was young, not much older than Mathilde. Kraal helped him to the ledge. "You're okay now," he said to the boy. "What's your name? You're not familiar to me."

"My name is Jahod," he said, clinging to Kraal. "Don't make me go back in there."

"That won't happen. We're going to get you out of here soon. We just have to free one more." Kraal swallowed hard. There were no more souls. The only way for Timothy to be free is if either Kraal or Tor sacrificed himself. Kraal understood what it meant. He understood why he had been bestowed such gifts. For this moment. But it still terrified him.

"I can't hear him," Tor said as Kraal approached. Tor choked back emotion. "Before, I could hear him, and now, there's nothing."

"I'm sorry," Kraal said quietly. "If I could go back, I would...I would have never taken you from your family."

"Just stop," Tor said, tears leaking from his eyes. Kraal tried not to act shocked, but he had never seen Tor like this. "I don't want your apologies! I just want my father! He shouldn't have to die like this!"

Kraal bent down and grabbed one of the vacated chains. "Come back for me when you find another soul." He placed the chain around his waist and walked to the edge of the abyss. "I trust you to come back for me, but I understand if you don't."

Before he stepped off the ledge, the chain rattled and fell at his feet. Kraal picked it up again and latched it in place. Just as before, it fell off. "It's not working," Kraal said in a panic. He didn't want to drop into the abyss without the chain. There'd be no coming back.

"Give me a hand," Tor said with a grunt.

Kraal stopped what he was doing to notice Tor pulling on the dangling chain with all his might. Moving quickly, Kraal joined him. When Kraal reached for the chain, his hand brushed Tor's. A shock of electricity went between them. "Whoa." Kraal felt the energy inside of him agree with Tor's. The two of them pulled on the chain and slowly they were able to pull it up.

"Don't stop," Tor said, but Kraal wasn't about to.

The two worked laboriously until they saw the top of Timothy's head. "I see him."

"Hold the chain steady." Tor moved to pull his father up the rest of the way.

Once Timothy was on the ledge, Kraal stopped pulling. Timothy wasn't moving.

"Father?" Tor said. "Timothy? Do you hear me? It's Tor."

Kraal watched as Tor felt Timothy's wrist. Tor grabbed his father and held him. "I'm right here. I need you to wake up. I'm right here."

Not knowing what else to do, Kraal knelt beside Tor and rested his hand on his shoulder. "I'm sorry."

Tor shoved Kraal's hand away. "Don't touch me! Get away. You did this!"

Kraal stood and stepped back, putting distance between them. While Tor began to openly weep, Kraal couldn't stop the tears from leaking from his own eyes. "I'm so sorry," he whispered. "I'm so sorry."

He felt a hand on his shoulder and turned to see Marcy beside him. "How did you do it? How'd the chain come up?"

"Tor threw Drakkon into the pit, and this Shadow boy came out. So, Tor and I yanked on the last chain until we got to Timothy."

Deborah frowned. "It was because his soul had left. The soul anchored him to the abyss while he lived. With him gone, his soul is no longer with us."

"He'll never forgive me."

"Trust me, Timothy is no longer in pain. There is no suffering where he's at. I know. It happened to me."

But Kraal didn't respond. None of it mattered. Because of him, Tor had lost both his parents.

"It's not your fault, Kraal. It's mine. I was supposed to protect Tor, but I failed."

"Did you kidnap Tor?" Kraal said bitterly. "No, I did, and then I tricked you into coming into hell. All of this is my fault. And now, Tor has lost his family."

"Everything has a purpose. Everything works out for the good. Everything. Even the messes we make. Think about it. Without you, we wouldn't have defeated Drakkon."

"It doesn't feel too good right now." Kraal wiped his eyes. The tears felt incredibly foreign to him, but he couldn't stop his eyes from leaking.

"Stay here for a sec, I need to be with Tor. We'll talk later, okay?" Marcy squeezed Kraal's shoulder and then walked over to Tor. But Tor shoved her off too.

"I don't want you here. Leave me alone."

"Tor, I'm sorry for your loss. I promise you his soul is no longer here in torment. He's been set free."

"Great, and I'm alone. Again."

"You are not alone. You have me and the others. You are free from Drakkon and this evil place."

"He needed me!" Tor was so distraught he brought his hands up to his hair and yanked. "I failed him!"

Deborah grabbed Tor and pulled him to her. He sobbed into her shoulder, and she let him. Kraal could only stand there and weep, letting the emotion overtake him too. "I'm so sorry," he would say, but no one was listening.

Eventually, Tor's tears depleted, and he pulled back from Deborah's arms. "I need to go."

Tor extended his hand and the red mist appeared. He tried to pick up his father, but he needed both hands to do it.

"Let me help." Kraal extended his arm. When his white mist appeared, Tor lifted his father, and without another look at Deborah or Kraal, he stepped through it. Deborah sighed, squeezed Kraal's arm, and followed Tor. Even though Kraal was tempted to leave them alone and go isolate himself somewhere, the energy inside him pushed for him to follow. So, he did, thankful that he at least would never have to go back to that evil place again.

TOR

Tor walked through the white mist and stepped into the abbey that had been Timothy's home. Tor had only ever observed the old building from the forest where he had stayed hidden when first arriving here with Lynde and Marcy. Well, Michael and Deborah. Whatever. But it was it's own sanctuary with wood floors and ceilings, rows of candles, and a large crucifix at the front. Tor understood the religious symbols, but none of that mattered as he held his lifeless father in his hands.

Michael walked into the building from a side door, holding it open. "We have something prepared," he said gently.

Tor nodded, not knowing what to do but to follow Michael.

The side door led to a small burial ground for the deceased. A spot had already been prepared for Timothy. Tor tried not to stare at the mound of dirt, knowing that in a few minutes that mound would be used to bury his father.

What Tor desired was to scream and rip his hair out and yell at all of them. But his father deserved better. And he'd give him that. He would bury him, and then he would leave. And never come back.

The ceremony Michael prepared was simple. The words were heartfelt, the prayer was powerful, and the energy inside Tor warmed him. But Tor was undeterred. Once the small group had walked away, he'd be gone.

Eventually, only Marcy and Kraal stayed, both kneeling beside him at the mound of dirt now covering his father's body. He tried not to be bitter toward them. Especially Marcy. She made him feel so many different ways, but right now, he wasn't thinking too clearly.

He understood that it was Drakkon who had his father taken and thrown into the abyss, but his entire horrific existence was because of these two, and he didn't feel like placating their guilt. They *needed* to feel guilty. This was just as much their fault as anyone else's. "Leave me alone," he said. "I'd like a minute to myself to grieve."

Marcy took his hand, and his heart betrayed him and began to pound. He looked into her blue eyes and nearly asked if she'd hold him again. But instead, he pulled his hand away and turned to stare glumly at the pile of dirt.

After they left, he rested his hand on top of the dirt. "I tried to save you," he whispered. "But I was too late. I let you down."

Tor heard someone approach and then kneel beside him. He opened his mouth to yell at them, but the person spoke first. "Would you like me to pray with you? You prayed with me once."

He turned to the familiar sound of his father's words. Timothy gave Tor a small smile. Tor's mouth hung open as he took in the vision in front of him. Timothy shone like Deborah, Samson, and

Eli. His gaze pierced into Tor, and his apparel was like the one Tor had found for himself. "You're a light-bearer," he finally said to his father.

Before Timothy responded, Tor wrapped his arms around him. "You're here. You're not dead."

"I'm not technically in my physical body anymore, but I'm not dead. I'm an eternal being, awarded the gift of light and protection."

Tor released him momentarily. "So, like Samson?"

"Yes," Timothy laughed. "I have been gifted with the inhabitation of this abbey."

"You are to protect it?"

"I'm to protect...*you*." When Tor didn't respond, Timothy continued, "It's incredible, Tor. Everything I read about this place, this feeling, it pales in comparison to the real thing. It all makes sense now. Everything that happened makes sense."

Tor lowered his gaze. "I'm glad it makes sense to you, but it doesn't to me. But I can't find the words to describe how relieved I am that you are here beside me."

"There's someone else who has been gifted with the inhabitation of this abbey." Timothy smiled. "Come with me."

Tor pushed himself up and followed Timothy back to the abbey. He wanted to keep reaching out and touching his father just to verify his presence. But he stopped when he reached the abbey's sanctuary and came face-to-face to a woman with a familiar face. His heart dropped at the sight of his mother. He took in the room and saw several angels surrounding them with Marcy and Kraal in the mix. All were grinning from ear-to-ear.

"Hello, my son," she said to Tor. "I've been waiting for this day for a long time."

Timothy leaned in and kissed his wife's cheek. "We are together again."

Tor approached her slowly. Her dark, curly hair had been pulled back and out of her face, making her eyes that much more beautiful. She shone, and not merely from being a newly appointed light-bearer, but there was something more, something powerful. Tor recognized it as love. She placed her hands on his shoulders and pulled him to her. The love poured through him, and for the first time in his life, Tor felt complete.

He felt Timothy's arms too and opened his arms to include him. The three of them stayed in an embrace for a long time. And for the first time, Tor understood what it felt like to have a family.

"I THOUGHT I'd find you here," Tor said, as he approached Marcy. She sat on the same bench overlooking the sea that she had not so long ago. "You like the view."

"I like it better from the sky, but I wanted to say good-bye before leaving. I thought this would be a nice place." She stood up and crossed her arms across her chest.

They stood close but not too close, neither one saying anything at first. There was much to say, yet both understood that it changed nothing. Their destinies were intertwined but not together.

"We've been through quite the ordeal," Tor said, breaking the silence. "It's hard to believe that it hasn't even been six mortal months since I was first assigned to kill you."

Marcy smiled. "Ah, yes, how can I forget?"

"I've put you through a lot," he said. "I'm sorry for that."

"Well, one could say I put you through a lot. And I'm sorry about that."

Tor turned and looked back at the abbey. Inside, his parents were in the large, communal kitchen cooking him dinner. This gift they'd been given had healed so many broken places of his heart. "If it hadn't been for you, I would have never met my mother. I would have died a prisoner in hell, stuck in hell for all eternity. I see it now." When he turned back to her, he saw her eyes wet with tears.

"I never thought about it like that."

"Neither had I. My mother reminded me of it. In hell, with all my bad decisions, my eternal soul would have been stuck in that inferno. You brought me out, and you gave me a chance to set things right."

"You've changed," Marcy said, shaking her head. "It's incredible, Tor. I can't even begin to tell you how happy it makes me to know you are safe here."

"Actually, I'm going to head back to Samson's sanctuary in the mountain. I've gotten close to him... and to Lin. I'd like him to keep training me. Something tells me that my powers are still going to be needed."

Marcy nodded in understanding. "Good. I'm glad."

"What about you? What are your and Michael's big plans?"

"We're going to lead the front lines together. As archangel and wife."

"So, this is more than just a good-bye because you're leaving, but it's a good-bye..." Tor stopped, not knowing what he was trying to say.

"Tor, I love you," she said simply. "I have since the moment I met you, which seems weird to fall in love in hell, but there it is. And

I still carry those feelings with me, and I always will. At first, I was upset. I wanted to forget them because of my love and commitment to Michael, but now, I'm glad that I've kept my memories and feelings while I was Marcy. You have made me better in so many ways."

"If anyone has made anyone else better, you have made me a better man than I thought could ever be possible. And I love you, Marcy. You'll always be Marcy to me."

"I know, and that's what has made my decision easier. Because to you, I will always be Marcy, and I understand that. But Tor, I am so much more. I am Deborah."

Tor took in the sight of her, truly understanding what she was saying. There was so much more to her than just those twenty years in hell, and Michael, as an eternal archangel, knew that and loved that about her. "I am happy you are to be wed. Is there a ceremony? In the mortal realm there are always celebrations."

"It's much simpler here on the side of the eternal."

"If you two come back for a visit, my parents will throw you a celebration. I'm sure of it." Tor smiled, trying to sound happier than he felt. He may understand the reasoning for her decision, but a big part of his heart would miss her terribly.

"Did I hear there's a celebration?" Timothy approached the two of them. "I love a good party."

"Marcy will be marrying Michael soon."

"It's Deborah," Marcy said gently.

Tor felt the heat on his face. "I don't know why I can't seem to get that right."

"Congratulations," Timothy said to Deborah. "We must throw you a party. It will be great fun, and we could use some fun around here."

Deborah grinned and shook her head. "I'm not sure. Let me check with Michael. I think he had the idea of simply whisking me away into the sunset."

There was an awkward pause before Deborah reached over and gave Tor a hug. "Until we meet again." She released him and hugged Timothy, then with a quick wave, shot straight up into the sky.

"You all right?" Timothy asked Tor.

"Surprisingly, yes." Tor stared up at the sky for another moment then looked at his father. "I love her, but I understand that it has to be this way."

"She and Michael were head over heels for each other before you came along. Talk about a hiccup."

"Well, she chose him, so no use staying upset about it. She said, I'd only ever see her as Marcy, and even though I hate to admit it, she's right. To me, she's Marcy. I never even bothered to call her anything different. But she's more than that, and Michael know it and loves her."

"And what about Kraal? Did he accept my offer?"

Tor kept his gaze on the ground. "Um…"

"You haven't talked to him yet, have you?"

"It's been busy."

"Nonsense, you're still avoiding him." Timothy wagged his finger at his son.

"It's complicated. What am I supposed to say?"

"Easy. You say that your parents would like to make him dinner. Simple." When Tor stayed quiet, Timothy added, "He saved the Shadows, Tor, and he saved you from those chains. It's time we let the past go."

"I know," Tor said. He noticed his father gave him a raised

eyebrow. "It's true! I do know that without Kraal we wouldn't have succeeded over Drakkon. I even think it's kind of cool that this whole prophecy about the human anomaly might have been about him and not me. It's just...hard for me to talk to him about it. Being raised in hell, saying the words forgiveness and mercy would get you beaten and thrown into a cage."

"We're not in hell anymore. Thank God. Now, let's go and chat with the young man who saved the day." Timothy rubbed his hands together and grinned.

"You are enjoying this light-bearer role a little too much," Tor teased.

"What? I get to teleport like Eli and Samson. And you! How cool is that?" He wiggled his eyebrows then disappeared.

Tor laughed and materialized in Eli's forest where many of the Shadows now recovered. Timothy already waited for him outside the cave.

That's where they'd find Kraal, helping the Shadows recover from the traumatic surgery.

"Let me talk to him first," Tor said. "If you don't mind?"

"Of course not," Timothy said. "I'll wait out here for a few minutes. Eli might need some help."

Tor stepped into the cave and vivid memories came back. This was where the evil seed had been ripped out of him. It's where he was taken when he nearly died at the hands of Drakkon. He spotted Kraal helping a Shadow drink from a small jug. "Do you need some help?" he asked Kraal.

"No, I'm good. He's the last one for a little bit." Kraal set down the jug. "How's your family?"

"Great. My parents want to invite you to a celebratory dinner in your honor."

Kraal's face fell. "Thank you, Tor, and I'm glad that it worked out for you to be with them again, but it's not because of me. Celebrate with each other, but I should stay out of it."

"Wait," Tor reached for Kraal. He took a deep breath, knowing that the words needed to come out. "I'm sorry, Kraal, for being so hard on you. For not forgiving you. It wasn't fair. Drakkon hurt my family. Not you. If you hadn't been successful in kidnapping me, Drakkon wouldn't have stopped until I was dead. Without you, we wouldn't have won. You helped me with the chains, and then you defeated Drakkon."

Kraal pressed his lips together and lowered his head. "It doesn't seem like enough, Tor. You were ripped away from your parents. I'm not sure that's forgivable."

"You wanted to be free. And I understand what that feels like. If I had stayed in the mortal realm, you and Marcy—I mean, Deborah —would have never crossed paths."

Kraal gave a slight nod. "If you say so."

"I do, and I insist you let my parents spoil you."

"I'm not too sure about that. Your mother only sees me as the one who stole her child."

"She doesn't see you that way at all," Timothy said. Tor hadn't realized he'd entered the cave. "She sees it as because of you Tor is alive and not chained in the pit. And we're grateful."

Kraal looked at Timothy, then at Tor, and smiled. "I'm not going to lie. It feels good to be forgiven."

Timothy and Tor agreed, and the three men together stepped out of the cave into the light of day.

EPILOGUE

KRAAL

He stepped outside, slowly shutting the front door of the old farmhouse. It had been abandoned and condemned, but to Kraal, it was home. Deborah had offered him to stay tucked in the sanctuary with Mathilde. All the Shadows released from the abyss chose freedom, and who could blame them? So, Michael and other angels divided them up to secret sanctuaries. Michael had warned that although most should make it, some would not. The Shadows didn't care. If it meant freedom from hell, they were willing to take that chance.

But this is where Kraal wanted to be. Deborah warned that mortal laws were in place and that the property technically belonged to someone. Kraal had walked into the human bank with her to inquire about the property. He had to remind himself to act normally. But what does normal look like? He found himself not making eye contact from years of hiding his eyes from mortals.

"Stop that," Deborah had whispered. "You look suspicious. You have to look people in the eye. That shows them you're trustworthy."

Come to find out, the property was part of the abbey's land. With Timothy's help, he completed the paperwork and agreed to pay rent to the abbey. Deborah joked that Kraal would need to find a job. He smiled at the idea. A human job? The thought fascinated him.

Timothy and Tor would arrive soon to help him with the renovation. Tor complained that he needed to get back to the mountains to train, but Kraal could see how much he enjoyed being with his family. And hey, Kraal would take all the help offered.

For now, he held a mug of coffee. Steam hit his face as he took a sip. He liked it with a little bit of sugar. He smiled down at it, remembering the first time he tried it. Timothy was a great guide for all things human.

The chill in the air would keep most people inside their homes, warmly tucked beneath their blankets in bed. But not Kraal. This was his favorite time of day. He looked out toward the eastern horizon as the sun just began to peak from its slumber. He'd never get enough of this. The beauty and marvel of a sunrise.

No longer a slave. Forever free.

Thank you for reading this book!

Mortal Realm Series:

Shadows of the Mortal Realm
Guardians of the Mortal Realm

Other books by Shay Lee Giertz:

Falling Too Deep
Lake Of Secrets